"It's late."

"It must be early somewhere in the world," Mindy said.

"Must be," Jason echoed.

But it was late here, and he had to keep that in mind. Just as he had to keep in mind that what he was feeling had no place in either of their lives right now. She was pregnant, he was her boss and they had both been badly burned by the people they'd chosen to spend their lives with. Not exactly great odds for starting a new relationship.

Still, a man was only so strong, had only so much within him to draw on to keep him noble. After that, it was every emotion for itself.

Just as it was now.

Gently threading his fingers through her hair, Jason tilted her face up toward his.

And kissed her.

The way they both wanted him to.

Dear Reader,

Step into warm and wonderful July with six emotional stories from Silhouette Special Edition. This month is full of heart-thumping drama, healing love and plenty of babies!

I'm thrilled to feature our READERS' RING selection, *Balancing Act* (SE#1552), by veteran Mills & Boon and Silhouette Romance author Lilian Darcy. This talented Australian writer delights us with a complex tale of a couple marrying for the sake of their twin daughters, who were separated at birth. The twins and parents are newly reunited in this tender and thought-provoking read. Don't miss it!

Sherryl Woods hooks readers with this next romance from her miniseries, THE DEVANEYS. In *Patrick's Destiny* (SE#1549), an embittered hero falls in love with a gentle woman who helps him heal a rift with his family. Return to the latest branch of popular miniseries, MONTANA MAVERICKS: THE KINGSLEYS, with *Moon Over Montana* (SE#1550) by Jackie Merritt. Here, an art teacher can't help but *moon over* a rugged carpenter who renovates her apartment—and happens to be good with his hands!

We are happy to introduce a multiple-baby-focused series, MANHATTAN MULTIPLES, launched by Marie Ferrarella with *And Babies Make Four* (SE#1551), which relates how a hardheaded businessman and a sweet-natured assistant, who loved each other in high school, reunite many years later and dive into parenthood. *His Brother's Baby* (SE#1553) by Laurie Campbell is the dramatic tale of a woman determined to take care of herself and her baby girl, but what happens when her baby's handsome uncle falls onto her path? In *She's Expecting* (SE#1554) by Barbara McMahon, an ambitious hero is wildly attracted to his new secretary—his new *pregnant* secretary—but steels himself from mixing business with pleasure.

As you can see, we have a lively batch of stories, delivering the very best in page-turning romance. Happy reading!

Sincerely,

Karen Taylor Richman
Senior Editor

Please address questions and book requests to:
Silhouette Reader Service
U.S.: 3010 Walden Ave., P.O. Box 1325, Buffalo, NY 14269
Canadian: P.O. Box 609, Fort Erie, Ont. L2A 5X3

And Babies Make Four

MARIE FERRARELLA

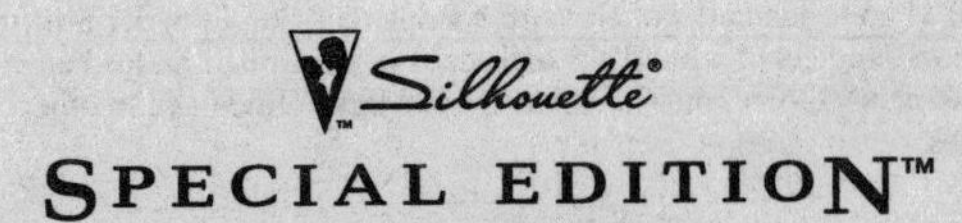

Published by Silhouette Books
America's Publisher of Contemporary Romance

Special thanks and acknowledgment are given to Marie Ferrarella for her contribution to the MANHATTAN MULTIPLES series.

To
Terry and Joe Unger,
for being the perfect hosts.

SILHOUETTE BOOKS

ISBN 0-373-24551-3

AND BABIES MAKE FOUR

This edition published by arrangement with Harlequin Books S.A.

Visit Silhouette at www.eHarlequin.com

Printed in U.S.A.

Books by Marie Ferrarella in Miniseries

ChildFinders, Inc.
A Hero for All Seasons IM #932
A Forever Kind of Hero IM #943
Hero in the Nick of Time IM #956
Hero for Hire IM #1042
An Uncommon Hero Silhouette Books
A Hero in Her Eyes IM #1059
Heart of a Hero IM #1105

Baby's Choice
Caution: Baby Ahead SR #1007
Mother on the Wing SR #1026
Baby Times Two SR #1037

Baby of the Month Club
Baby's First Christmas SE #997
Happy New Year—Baby! IM #686
The 7lb., 2oz. Valentine Yours Truly
Husband: Optional SD #988
Do You Take This Child? SR #1145
Detective Dad World's Most Eligible Bachelors
The Once and Future Father IM #1017
In the Family Way Silhouette Books
Baby Talk Silhouette Books
An Abundance of Babies SE #1422

Like Mother, Like Daughter
One Plus One Makes Marriage SR #1328
Never Too Late for Love SR #1351

The Bachelors of Blair Memorial
In Graywolf's Hands IM #1155
M.D. Most Wanted IM #1167
Mac's Bedside Manner SE #1492
Undercover M.D. IM #1191

Two Halves of a Whole
The Baby Came C.O.D. SR #1264
Desperately Seeking Twin Yours Truly

Those Sinclairs
Holding Out for a Hero IM #496
Heroes Great and Small IM #501
Christmas Every Day IM #538
Caitlin's Guardian Angel IM #661

The Cutlers of the Shady Lady Ranch
Fiona and the Sexy Stranger Yours Truly
Cowboys Are for Loving Yours Truly
Will and the Headstrong Female Yours Truly
The Law and Ginny Marlow Yours Truly
A Match for Morgan Yours Truly
A Triple Threat to Bachelorhood SR #1564

***The Reeds**
Callaghan's Way IM #601
Serena McKee's Back in Town IM #808

***McClellans & Marinos**
Man Trouble SR #815
The Taming of the Teen SR #839
Babies on His Mind SR #920
The Baby Beneath the Mistletoe SR #1408

***The Alaskans**
Wife in the Mail SE #1217
Stand-In Mom SE #1294
Found: His Perfect Wife SE #1310
The M.D. Meets His Match SE #1401
Lily and the Lawman SE #1467

***The Pendletons**
Baby in the Middle SE #892
Husband: Some Assembly Required SE #931

The Mom Squad
A Billionaire and a Baby SE #1528
A Bachelor and a Baby SD #1503
The Baby Mission IM #1220
Beauty and the Baby SR #1668

*Unflashed series

MARIE FERRARELLA

earned a master's degree in Shakespearean comedy, and, perhaps as a result, her writing is distinguished by humor and natural dialogue. This RITA® Award-winning author's goal is to entertain and to make people laugh and feel good. She has written over one hundred books for Silhouette, some under the name Marie Nicole. Her romances are beloved by fans worldwide and have been translated into Spanish, Italian, German, Russian, Polish, Japanese and Korean.

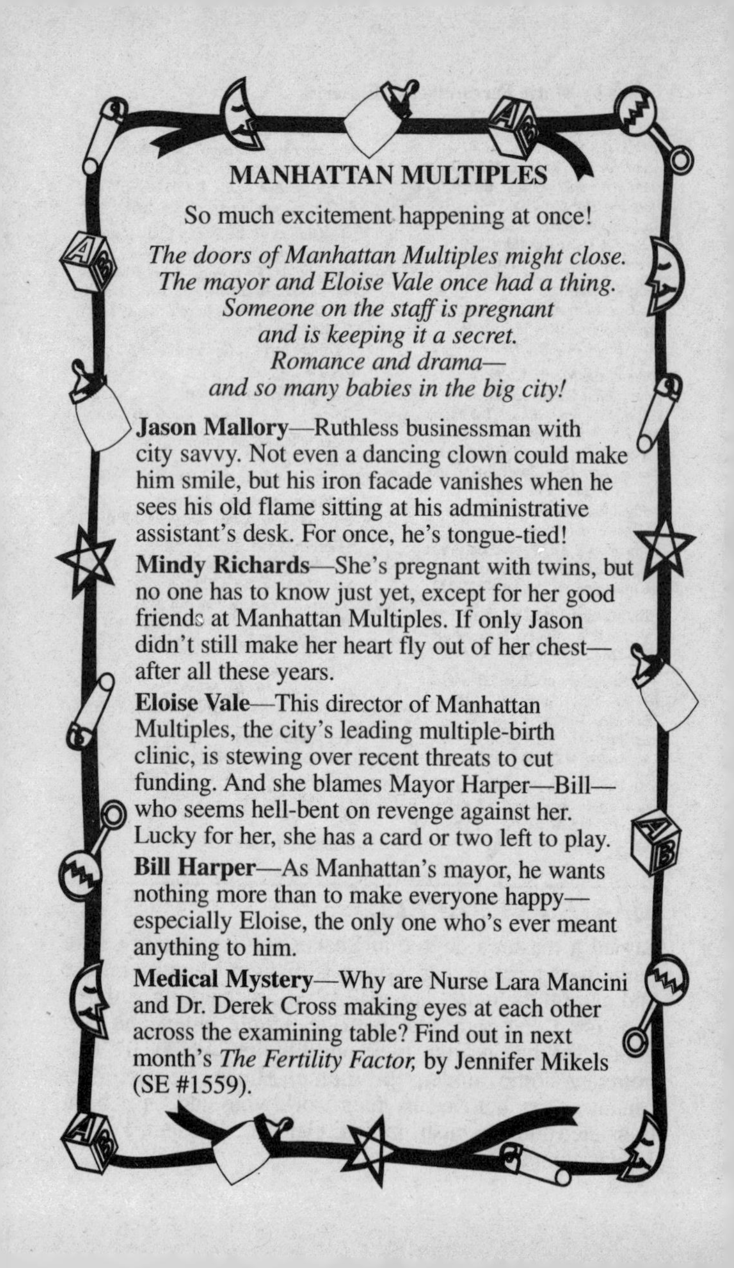

MANHATTAN MULTIPLES

So much excitement happening at once!

The doors of Manhattan Multiples might close.
The mayor and Eloise Vale once had a thing.
Someone on the staff is pregnant
and is keeping it a secret.
Romance and drama—
and so many babies in the big city!

Jason Mallory—Ruthless businessman with city savvy. Not even a dancing clown could make him smile, but his iron facade vanishes when he sees his old flame sitting at his administrative assistant's desk. For once, he's tongue-tied!

Mindy Richards—She's pregnant with twins, but no one has to know just yet, except for her good friends at Manhattan Multiples. If only Jason didn't still make her heart fly out of her chest—after all these years.

Eloise Vale—This director of Manhattan Multiples, the city's leading multiple-birth clinic, is stewing over recent threats to cut funding. And she blames Mayor Harper—Bill—who seems hell-bent on revenge against her. Lucky for her, she has a card or two left to play.

Bill Harper—As Manhattan's mayor, he wants nothing more than to make everyone happy—especially Eloise, the only one who's ever meant anything to him.

Medical Mystery—Why are Nurse Lara Mancini and Dr. Derek Cross making eyes at each other across the examining table? Find out in next month's *The Fertility Factor,* by Jennifer Mikels (SE #1559).

Prologue

"Why that no-good so-and-so."

Grabbing up the newspaper from her desk, Eloise Vale narrowly avoided tipping over her coffee cup and sending a creamy, off-brown river pooling over the exact article she wanted to read. The one that announced that the ever-dapper, much-sought-after mayor of New York, Bill Harper, once *her* Bill Harper until she'd come to her senses, was debating overwhelming budget cuts in order to balance the city's budget. Budget cuts that would, in addition to other things, cripple a great many much-needed charitable programs. *Her* program was on the list of possibilities.

Ignoring her newly rescued coffee, Eloise sat staring at the article, the words bouncing off her eyes like so many misfired photon torpedoes, her stomach cramping up as it wound itself into one huge knot.

There it was, Manhattan Multiples, smack in the middle. The mayor might as well have placed a gun to her head. Or her heart.

"How could he?" she demanded out loud of the cool pastel-blue walls that surrounded her Madison Avenue office.

Her office was the very hub that was Manhattan Multiples, an organization that had begun as a support group championed by one lone woman. Manhattan Multiples had grown like the proverbial weed until it had mushroomed into a foundation occupying three floors of the ten-story building. Rather than just a single small group of people, it now encompassed services that ranged from support groups—including career counseling, Lamaze, yoga and meditation classes—not to mention a thriving day-care center, all for women faced with the frightening and overwhelming reality of giving birth to not just one life-changing child, but two or more.

Eloise knew what that was all about. She'd had to face up to it herself when she'd given birth to her three boys, now all entering their adolescence together, a state guaranteed to turn her ash-blond hair as gray as her eyes. She hadn't had a clue how to handle the situation, not then. And she wouldn't have had much more than a hint now if it wasn't for the organization she'd started and now oversaw, an organization blessed with knowledgeable people who came to share their experiences, their advice and their acquired wisdom with women who were scared out of their minds.

''And he wants to pull the plug on us?'' Eloise drew the newspaper closer as she looked at the face of the man she had almost married instead of Walter. ''Think again, Billy-boy. If you think I'm capitulating without one hell of a fight, boy have you got the wrong woman.''

With a pronounced sigh, Eloise threw the paper aside and picked up her coffee.

Chapter One

That Monday morning Jason Mallory had a great many things on his mind as he hurried into the spacious suite that comprised the securities investment offices of Mallory and Dixon. From the ridiculous—as in where he'd stashed his dry cleaning ticket for a jacket he needed—to the sublime, which meant going over the net-quarterly returns of a very successful firm season.

Being instantly and unceremoniously catapulted into the past, however, was not one of them.

But, scheduled or not, that was exactly where he found himself. In the past. More than eleven years in the past to be exact, at a time when he had been the loner in a local high school where everyone else seemed to know one another.

At that time, all he'd had were his thoughts, his books and an overwhelming ambition to become someone. A powerful "someone." Someone a person like Mindy Conway would notice. She'd been, as much as anything, the reason why he'd been so driven, so compelled to scale those corporate mountains, so dedicated to accumulating not only money but respect for who and what he was.

She had been his catalyst, his focus. His impossible dream, even after she'd left town. Because loners like him didn't stand a chance with popular girls like Mindy Conway.

So, after high school, after she'd gone away to Northwestern, he'd stayed in New York and attended first NYU, then Columbia University. And diligently worked toward his goal even though he would never see Mindy again.

After a while, of course, there had been Debra. Debra, with her extensive family connections that she'd tried to dangle before him like some kind of enticement. Debra with her sexy smile and her own agenda. Why she'd chosen to single him out as the man she wanted to be with was still a mystery to him. A flattering mystery.

At least, it was flattering at first.

But that all changed once vows had been exchanged and for the first time in his life, he'd surrendered himself completely to a woman, breaking down his own walls of reserve to be the man he thought she wanted him to be. He'd thought wrong. And just as suddenly as she'd burst onto his horizon, she'd withdrawn from it. From him. Physically, emotionally. He had no clue as to why. Another mystery, one he chose not to explore. The pain there was still too great. And very possibly always would be, he judged.

But now, for some strange, whimsical reason known only to the gods who helmed the universe strictly for their own amusement, the girl from his long-lost past was here. In his office.

Sitting at a desk.

Mindy.

Bigger than life and twice as beautiful as he remembered.

But Mindy wasn't a girl anymore, she was a woman. A gorgeous woman with longish, straight black hair and the most beautiful sky-blue eyes he'd ever seen.

And he wasn't that quiet, introverted loner no one noticed. He was Jason Mallory, whose business acumen people listened to with rapt attention because in this strange, topsy-turvy world of upending finances, he somehow, through instinct and a great deal of careful observation and painstaking, ongoing evaluation, knew how to negotiate through the often turbulent and troubled waters of the stock market.

Right now he would rather have been traveling down the Colorado white rapids in a canoe made out of paper cups than standing here, staring at a woman who could have so easily had his heart—if she had only known that he was alive.

For a frozen second in time, Jason's mouth felt too dry to form any words.

A single word kept echoing within Mindy Richards's brain over and over again, each time increasing in volume. Omigod, omigod, OMIGOD!

She was surprised that she'd somehow managed to keep it tucked in the confines of her head and not let it burst out of her all-but-numbed lips.

It was a complete set. Her numbed lips went with her numbed everything else. Because that's how she felt. Completely numbed. She'd become that way the second she raised her eyes to see who walked in through the door of the office that she had only moments ago walked into herself.

Everything inside of her froze for exactly half a beat, then went into a frenzied dance, the kind that would make a musician's fingers fall off if he tried to emulate it.

Forget about what her heart was doing.

Jason? Jason Mallory?

It just hadn't occurred to her that the Mallory attached to the logo on the door belonged to Jason, to the hunk she'd spent all four of her high school years daydreaming about. How many hours had she wasted wishing, praying, that he would part the sea of people in the high school hallway and just walk up to her? She couldn't begin to remember.

All she remembered was that he hadn't made that short trip. And she hadn't had the nerve to approach him. Except on the very last day of high school, when, clutching her senior yearbook to her young chest, she'd walked up to Jason and asked him to sign it for her. The words had tasted like cotton in her mouth, but she'd gotten them out somehow. And belatedly remembered to smile.

Have A Nice Life—Jason. That was all he'd written. It was enough. She'd slept with the open page beside her on her pillow for weeks.

Right now, remembering how she'd felt approaching him that one time infused a ray of heat through her that melted away the iciness of her fingertips. She had to remember to make herself breathe.

Eventually, after she'd gone to Northwestern in pursuit of a degree in journalism, Jason had become that unattainable star for her, like some celebrity you fall in love with on the screen. With effort, she'd filed him away in her mind. To take out and sneak a peek at every so often when her spirits were low and she needed to think, "What if—?"

But that was before Brad had entered her life. "What if—" became a thing of the past. Until just recently. She had no idea why, but as she'd spent her first night in her new, minuscule apartment, she'd found herself thinking what if Jason had taken that single opportunity to talk to her? What if they'd gone out, become romantically involved and gotten married? What if they'd begun their married life in an apartment just like this little bit of plaster, floorboard and paint?

God, but life was funny. She'd never dreamed that

she'd run into him again. Yet, here he was, looking twice as gorgeous as he ever had.

Jason thought he was hallucinating. Maybe the pressure he'd been putting on himself had finally gotten to him. Like a man not entirely sure of what his eyes were seeing, he said her name. Part of him expected her to either vanish or transform into someone else, into the real woman sitting there.

''Mindy?''

She couldn't think, couldn't even answer in the affirmative. All she could do was say his name. And hope that she didn't sound like some addle-brained idiot. ''Jason?''

Somehow he found enough moisture in his mouth to ask, ''What are you doing here?''

Even as Jason asked the question, he upbraided himself. Damn it, he sounded just as tongue-tied as he was certain he would have if he'd ever tried to talk to her in high school. What the hell was wrong with him? He gave seminars for high-ranking financiers from all over the country without so much as a second's hesitation. Met with important CEOs of major companies on a regular basis. Even if this *was* Mindy, there was no reason to feel as if the very foundation of his life had suddenly transformed into delicately arranged playing cards.

He followed up his own question with the only thing he could think of. ''Are you here for some financial advice?''

But if that were the case, what was she doing, sitting at the desk normally occupied by the battalion of temporary administrative assistants his partner, Nathalie Dixon, kept insisting on hiring?

Her eyes never left his face. *My God but he'd gotten even sexier looking than I remembered. Stop it, you can't think like that anymore.*

"No," Mindy heard herself saying, "I work here."

Jason frowned. He'd only been away on business for four days. "Since when?"

"Since now." That sounded almost confrontational, she thought as a sudden zip of panic came out of nowhere. "Um—" she looked at her wristwatch, wanting to be more accurate "—since ten minutes ago."

His dark-brown eyes narrowed beneath what Mindy had always considered to be perfectly shaped eyebrows. She couldn't help wondering if her heightened hormonal state was responsible for her very physical, very intense reaction to Jason.

"I don't understand." When he'd left Wednesday evening, the young, rather vapid temp who'd been sitting at this desk was gathering her things together to leave. Permanently. He'd just assumed that Nathalie would find someone else from that bottomless well of temps. How did Mindy Conway even remotely qualify?

Mindy knew she had to get control of the butterflies that were dive bombing around her as-yet visually undetectable twins or she was going to make an absolute fool of herself and throw up right in front of

Jason. Trying to pull herself above this newest unforeseen wrinkle in her life, Mindy pressed a hand to her stomach, hoped he wouldn't notice this very maternal gesture and tried to sound as professional as possible under the circumstances. "Ms. Dixon hired me."

"Oh, she did, did she?" Jason raised his voice as he called out his partner's name, "Nathalie."

The effort wasn't necessary. His learned and usually very levelheaded business partner, not to mention close friend—at least up to this point—materialized in the doorway of her office which was next to his. There was an amused expression he didn't appreciate creasing Nathalie's lips.

"I see you've met our new administrative assistant." Nathalie's eyes shifted from Jason's handsome, tanned face and almost permanent sober expression to the rather shocked look on their new employee's face. Nathalie sighed. "Oh, God, Jason, you're not frightening the help already, are you?" She offered Mindy a broad smile. "Because I picked this one to last."

In response, Jason took hold of Nathalie's arm, mumbled a barely audible "excuse us" to Mindy and shepherded his partner into her office. He managed to shut the door before demanding, "What the hell are you doing?"

Jason and she went back a ways, back to the first elementary business course at Columbia. She'd begun her education later than most and because of their age difference, treated Jason like a younger brother who needed occasional emotional support. She'd seen him through his wedding and the unsteady years that followed, and she knew him as well as, if not better than, anyone.

"Trying to run an efficient office while you make predictions from the top of Mt. Sinai, my friend, why?" She seemed to scrutinize his face, as if trying to discern what was really up. "We decided to split the tasks, remember? I was going to handle the mundane things, like getting the office to run in a timely fashion and schmooze with the clients while you were going to handle the research that has made our company a household name among the famous and rich who want desperately to remain that way." She glanced past his shoulder toward where the outer office was. "Now, Mindy Richards seems like a very bright, capable young woman who just needs a chance to show us her stuff without being raked over the coals in the first ten seconds of your entrance."

Richards? Was she married? It occurred to him that he hadn't looked at her hand. He'd been too stunned to look at anything but her face.

Of course she was married. Probably in the first ten minutes after graduation. Someone like Mindy had her pick of men.

He couldn't bank down the feeling of sadness that suddenly rose up and filled him.

Nathalie was looking at him as if he was some kind of science experiment that had gone awry. He forced his mind forward. ''How could you hire her without asking me?''

''Simple. I never asked you before. And,'' she reminded him diplomatically, in case he missed this salient point, ''I never said very much when you sent them all fleeing into the hills. But I swear, Jason, you send this one packing and we are going to have a very, very serious talk about adjusting this attitude of yours.'' Her voice softened a little. ''I know where this is coming from, but it's been over a year since—''

The look in his eyes was the darkest she'd ever seen. It cut her off midbreath.

''That has *nothing* to do with it.'' Nathalie was closer to him than anyone else ever had been, but even she was not allowed to cross a certain line.

''It has *everything* to do with it. With you and the way you've become.''

Jason could feel himself shutting down. Even if he wanted to, he couldn't bring himself to discuss Debra's death or the effect it had on him. Just as he couldn't talk about how the empty sham of a marriage had unmanned him. ''Drop it, Nat.''

She sighed. Stubborn though she was, even she knew when to stop hitting her head against a brick wall.

''All right—for now. And only because we both have work to do,'' she added in case he thought he'd won. ''But I want you to behave around that girl, hear me? She needs this job.''

Why, he wondered. Why would Mindy need a job that was so completely out of the realm of what she'd gone to school for? And if she was married, wouldn't her husband be able to provide for her so that she could find work in her field?

It didn't make any sense to him.

Jason looked at his partner. "Why?"

Nathalie stared at him. "Since when do you care about the personal life of anyone?"

"That's not fair." Damn it, she made him sound like some kind of self-absorbed despot. Feeling unaccountably restless, he shoved his hands into the pockets of his Italian custom-made slacks.

"All right, it's not. You've been good to me." Reaching up, Nathalie placed her arm around his shoulder in big-sister fashion. "But I worry about you, Jason," she confessed. "About what all this enforced solitude is doing to you."

He knew she meant well, but he wasn't in the mood for this. He shrugged off her arm. "I just got back from a convention of three thousand people—"

"It's very easy to be alone in a crowded room. All you need is a mind that isolates you." Tilting her head, she studied him for a moment. Then her eyes widened as a realization seemed to come with the suddenness of a fireworks display on the Fourth of July. "You know her, don't you?" When he made no immediate denial, she advanced to the next plateau. "What is she, an old girlfriend? Someone you had a wild, secret fling with?" The grin nearly split her face. "Oh, Jason, I didn't think you had it in you."

"I don't. I didn't." Damn it, where did she get off, making these wild assumptions? Well-meaning or not, sometimes Nathalie really got on his nerves. "She's just someone I used to know."

She cocked her head. "Know how, in the biblical sense?"

"In the elementary sense, as in high school. We went to the same school, that's all," he emphasized. He peeled off his jacket. It was suddenly very warm in the office. "Get your mind out of the gutter, Nat."

"Don't be so judgmental, Jason. Under the right set of circumstances, the gutter can be a very nice place to visit once in a while." The wink she sent his way was a broad one. Nathalie cleared her throat. "All right, so now that we've established that this is a prior mysterious acquaintance—"

Damn it, why did she insist on digging this way? "Not mysterious, Nathalie, I just told you—"

She was quick to cut him off. "Oh, but it's what you *didn't* tell me that I'm more interested in, Jason. One doesn't look like that if one runs into the kid who sat beside you in homeroom and once borrowed your pen so they could finish their English homework." The look she gave him was a knowing one and all the more infuriating for it. Nathalie had never cared for Debra, although he'd found that out only after the fact. And she had been trying her damnedest to get him to go out again no matter how often he told her to butt out of that part of his life. "I'd wager there was more to it than that."

"Then you'd lose, Nathalie."

"I never lose." Nathalie tossed her head, sending her vibrant auburn hair cascading over her shoulder. "I just suffer temporary setbacks that will eventually be overcome if I just hang in there." It was a great motto for a firm that specialized in stock market finances. It was also the motto that Nathalie lived by.

"Excuse me, is anything wrong?"

In unison, they turned around to the source of the question. To the young woman standing now in the open doorway.

Self-conscious, Mindy dropped her hand to her side. "I knocked—twice—but I guess you didn't hear me," she explained.

Mindy had sat at her desk, pretending she didn't hear the raised voices or that her future might not very well be hanging in the balance with what was being said. But it was. Since she'd arrived back in New York, she'd gone to a score of companies in response to almost any ad she found in the paper that didn't list working out in the open fields in its job description. In desperation, she would have even gone for that, but her present stamina wouldn't allow it. The tone of the interviews that had been conducted all wound up being the same. Hopefully positive, until her own code of honor forced her to be truthful with her perspective employer and admit that, although she didn't look it, she was three months pregnant with twins.

And really, really needed this job, she would add silently.

Granted her parents were more than willing to take her in, but that wasn't the way she wanted to start her new life here—indebted to her parents. It was enough that they gave her emotional support and had floated her a loan so that she could put down the first and last month's sccurity on her tiny apartment. The latter was the size of a moderate walk-in restaurant refrigerator, but it was hers and that meant a lot. So did earning her own way.

Up until this job, no one had room for a woman who was going to expand before their eyes in the coming months and whom they felt might or might not be back once she gave birth, despite all her assurances that she would be. But Nathalie Dixon had been sympathetic and understanding and willing to take a chance on her, which meant the world to Mindy. She'd instantly taken a liking to the other woman.

But it was obvious that she was going to have to convince the man from her past that she was up to this. Funny how things turned out.

She wondered how much Nathalie had told him. But Jason's eyes weren't traveling to her belly, so maybe he didn't know.

Which was just the way she wanted it for now. One battle at a time.

"No," Jason said curtly, sparing a look at Nathalie before he turned to face Mindy, "nothing's wrong. Let's see about getting you to work, Mindy."

She smiled, relieved. Maybe this was going to be all right after all. "That sounds good to me."

We'll see, Jason added silently. We'll see.

Chapter Two

Jason glanced at his watch. It was nearly five o'clock. Finally. All day it had felt as if the minutes were dragging on the back of an arthritic turtle.

He hadn't been able to concentrate for more than ten, fifteen of those slow-moving minutes at a time. No matter how hard he tried to block out everything, his mind kept wandering back to the woman sitting some thirty feet outside of his office.

His lack of self-discipline surprised and annoyed him. It had been years since he hadn't been able to throw a rope around his thoughts and rein them in.

He had even managed to contain the pain and guilt he felt over Debra's death, placing the emotions in a sealed area so that he could get on with his work.

That had been the important thing then. Work had been his main goal, his main purpose for existing and his salvation, all wrapped up in one—much to the relief of the great many investors that his company handled who had come to depend very heavily on his knowledge and his savvy.

Without him a lot of people would have found themselves adrift in financial waters that seemed to keep insisting on changing course without giving the slightest warning to them.

He wasn't much good to any of them now, least of all himself, Jason thought darkly, thoroughly disgusted with himself.

With a sigh he closed the folder containing the reports he'd been staring at without success for the past half hour. Pushing away from the desk, he dragged a hand through his hair.

The July sun was shining brightly into his window, and he caught a glimpse of his reflection in the glass. He doubted that anyone looking at him would have had a clue what was going on inside of him, just as they wouldn't have been able to tell back in the days when he was in high school. He'd learned early on how to mask his feelings from the outside world.

But that didn't make them any less real to him.

This had to stop, he told himself. But at the moment, he didn't see how. It couldn't end by dismissing Mindy. He hadn't expected it, but she was good. She'd taken to the work like a proverbial duck to water, absorbing everything he said. Unlike with the temps who had paraded through the office, he hadn't had to explain anything to her twice. What was more, she didn't act as if he was speaking in some unfathomable foreign language. The world of finance left a great many people anesthetized, but Mindy just looked at him with those bright-blue eyes of hers, and he could see she understood. In his book, that made her a very rare person.

But then, he already knew that.

Jason massaged his forehead. The shadow of a headache was playing hide-and-seek with his temples, threatening to take over. What he needed, he thought, was a stiff drink. He didn't indulge often, but this definitely felt like one of those times men announced that they needed a drink.

Nerve endings tightened as he heard the knock on his door. Nathalie rarely knocked, she just strolled in. The fact that it could be one of the interns whom he kept to pore over every bit of news data that affected the market, never even occurred to him.

He knew it was *her*. "Come in."

And he was right. The next moment Mindy was standing in the doorway, her hand resting on the doorknob, a somewhat uncertain expression on her face.

He wasn't accustomed to seeing her that way. The Mindy Conway he remembered was the last word in confidence, in vibrancy.

But she wasn't Mindy Conway anymore, she was Mindy Richards, he reminded himself.

Looking at her now, it seemed as if someone had

put out her light, and she was struggling to strike at least a small match again.

What had happened to her? he wondered.

Mindy cleared her throat. The last time she'd felt this awkward, she'd accidentally put on two different-colored shoes and hadn't realized it until she was halfway to class.

"Um, it's five o'clock and I was going to..."

The words didn't feel right even as she said them. They felt stilted on her tongue. Everything since she'd walked in on Brad, in his plush insurance office, body wrestling with his secretary, had felt stilted to her. As though she was walking around in someone else's dream.

Or someone else's nightmare. It certainly wasn't hers.

Mindy bit her lower lip and tried again. The words still didn't feel right. Or maybe it was just the situation. Here she was, playing office with someone she'd once envisioned dressed only in a loincloth. She'd heard from someone in high school that Jason had a killer body. She had a feeling he still did.

"I was wondering, will there be anything else before I go home, um, Mr. Mallory?"

She saw him frown. Had she said something wrong? When he'd given her instructions today he'd been even more reserved than she'd remembered. At least back in high school she'd caught him looking her way occasionally. Enough times to set her heart racing. This time he was acting as if she was some kind of annoyance he was forced to deal with because of circumstances.

Jason's frowned deepened at her use of his last name. The chasm between them felt even wider than before. ''Don't call me that.''

She pressed her lips together. ''What should I call you?''

''Jason.'' He fairly snapped out his own name.

She tilted her head slightly as if considering the directive. And then she shook it. ''But you're my boss, it doesn't seem right.''

He laughed shortly, the words escaping before he could think them through. ''It doesn't seem right me being your boss.''

''Are you going to fire me?'' Her breath made a pit stop in her throat and stayed there.

He looked as her as if she'd just suggested his alter ego was Spiderman. ''What gave you that idea?''

Was it going to be like this every day? Was she going to feel horribly uncomfortable every time she was in his presence? She'd tried her damnedest today to be bright and cheery and eager, hoping to win him over, but he'd just seemed to become progressively worse every time he talked to her.

Mindy felt as if she was digging a deeper hole for herself with every word she uttered. But she had no choice but to respond. ''Well, for one thing, you're frowning.''

''He always frowns.''

Mindy almost sighed with relief as she heard Nathalie's voice behind her. Turning, she saw the woman pausing in the doorway, obviously on her way out.

Nathalie's eyes were smiling as she turned them toward her. "You know how when you were a kid and your mother warned you not to make funny faces because it would freeze that way? Jason didn't listen." With a throaty laugh at her own joke, Nathalie patted her on the shoulder. "Just wanted to tell you you did a great job today, Mindy. Keep it up." She looked significantly at Jason. "Well, I have to go. I've got a date," she announced.

Jason glanced at his calendar, as if to assure himself that this was Monday, the beginning of a work week. "A date?"

"Yes, a date."

Nathalie leaned into the office, her eyes on Jason. She tossed her hair, obviously knowing the lighting would catch some of the red highlights her hairdresser had slaved to put in.

"Some of us have a social life." She winked at her partner. "See you tomorrow, smiley."

Nodding at Mindy, she sailed out of the room and out of the suite of offices.

Nathalie left silence in her wake. Jason shifted in his seat. He and Nathalie needed to have a long talk soon about her less-than-subtle hints.

"Well, you're probably in a hurry to get to your husband, so I'll see you tomorrow." He was already looking down at the report he couldn't seem to read.

She was being dismissed, Mindy thought. A lot better than being fired. Still, something wouldn't allow her to leave this way. "That won't be possible."

Jason raised his eyes from his reading material and caused a tidal wave in her stomach. She hoped the twins were able to grab on to something stable to weather the storm out.

"I won't see you tomorrow?"

"No, I mean it won't be possible for me to hurry to my husband."

Having gone through the trauma himself, the first thing that occurred to Jason was that her spouse was dead. And he'd just told her to hurry off home to him. Quickly he tried to make amends.

"Hey, I'm sorry—"

She had no idea why he felt he had to apologize. "Nothing for you to be sorry about." Unable to stop it, the mental image of Brad's limbs tangled around that two-bit, anorexic flake he'd supposedly hired to take dictation flashed across her brain. "Brad, of course, is another story."

Damn, why had she just said that? Mindy upbraided herself. Jason certainly didn't want to hear about her life and she certainly didn't want to talk about it. From the way he was acting, Jason didn't want to hear about anything that had to do with anything that was outside of the company he ran.

He surprised her by leaning forward. "What do you mean?"

Panic nibbled away at her, followed by a wave of

shame. Her husband had cheated on her. Not once, but a number of times. This after she'd tried so hard to please him. Had given up so much to make him happy. That meant there had to be something lacking in her. She didn't want Jason to think that, didn't want to see pity in his eyes. "You don't want to hear."

"I wouldn't have asked the question if I didn't want to hear an answer." He leaned back in his chair, allowing himself to study Mindy for the first time. Along with the beauty, there were signs of stress that artful applications of makeup didn't completely manage to hide. What did she have to be stressed about? What had happened to her since the years they walked the same halls together? "What are you doing here, Mindy?"

She raised her chin ever so slightly. Defensiveness rose in her chest. "Working."

"Besides that."

She glanced toward the doorway that Nathalie had just vacated. "Trying to go home."

Jason sighed. What had come over him? Where did he get off, prying? He'd never appreciated probing questions aimed at him. The least he could do was treat her the way he wanted to be treated.

He waved her on her way. "Sorry, didn't mean to keep you."

This time the dismissal stung. She hadn't meant to shut him out. "No, I'm sorry. That wasn't very polite of me. You asked a question and I gave you a flippant answer." She squared her shoulders. "The reason I'm not going home to my husband is because I'm divorced, or about to be,'' she amended. The divorce was almost final. It couldn't be fast enough for her.

Divorced. He and Debra would have been divorced by now if she hadn't been killed. A wave of empathy washed over him. ''Oh. I'm sorry.''

Oh no, was that pity in his eyes? She wasn't about to accept pity, not even from the hunk who'd inhabited her daydreams for so long. If possible, she squared her shoulders even farther. A tiny ache rose instantly in her lower back. A sign of things to come, she thought. But first things first.

''I'm not.'' She glanced at her watch. If she hurried, she could just make her five forty-five appointment with her doctor at Manhattan Multiples.

He saw the way she looked at her watch. He was keeping her, he thought, and she was anxious to get away. Jason inclined his head. ''I'll see you tomorrow.''

It was her cue to go. Still, she paused one moment longer. She needed to know. ''Then it was all right? My work?''

''Your work was fine. Surprisingly so.'' He saw her brows narrow. She probably took that as an insult, he realized, and was quick to make himself clear. ''I didn't think this kind of thing was up your alley.''

She was grateful for the presence of mind that had made her take business courses while at Northwestern. ''Survival is up everyone's alley.''

''No argument there.'' He closed the folder for the

last time that day. No use beating a stalled horse. ''And Mindy—''

She turned from the door to look at him over her shoulder. ''Yes?''

''Tomorrow call me Jason. Mr. Mallory makes me feel like my old man.''

There was nothing old about Jason, she thought. Godlike, maybe, but not old. ''Fine. Jason, then.''

Mindy smiled to herself. Workplace or not, it felt right calling him that. Like something had just moved closer in sync.

With that she withdrew, unaware that he watched her progress all the way to the front door. Or that he continued to look at the door, lost in thought, for a long while after that.

''You can sit up now.''

Digging her elbows in closer to her body, Mindy pushed herself up from the examination table. She sat up, dangling her legs over the side. She looked at the rugged profile of her doctor, Derek Cross, and realized that she was holding her breath. These days she kept waiting for the shoes to fall and disasters to line themselves up like macabre ducks in a row. His expression gave nothing away, short of the fact that he looked tired.

''Is everything all right, Dr. Cross? With the babies, I mean,'' she added when he looked at her.

''Couldn't be better.'' He retired his stethoscope, draping the length of it along his neck while his nurse,

Lara Mancini, removed the machine that had allowed Mindy to listen to the heartbeats of the babies she was carrying. They sounded like tiny hoofbeats. Looking at his patient, he smiled. "But I'm afraid you're going to have to prepare yourself to be losing that girlish figure of yours very soon."

She'd forgotten about that. Mindy bit her lower lip, her thoughts shifting to Jason as if they were on automatic pilot. She wasn't normally a vain person, but this time it was different. This time she was going to be facing Jason. She wanted at least a little time before she mushroomed.

"Am I going to be huge?"

Derek exchanged glances with Lara and laughed. "Not if you don't take your condition to mean you have carte blanche at the dinner table. If you eat sensibly and exercise, there's absolutely no reason for you to gain much more weight than what these babies of yours will come to on their own."

Exercise. Didn't Manhattan Multiples have a gym on the premises? "How much exercise?"

Flipping to a new page within her chart, Derek began to make some notes to himself. "Well, I wouldn't go hang gliding in the desert anytime soon, but within reason you can continue whatever you're accustomed to." He glanced up at her. "One of my patients played tennis until the end of her eighth month. Of course, she wasn't carrying twins. Don't push yourself but don't baby yourself, either, no pun intended."

"Don't let him kid you," Lara interjected, grinning

as she continued tidying up within the room, "Dr. Cross intended it."

"A nurse is supposed to back up her doctor." Derek managed to keep a straight face only long enough to get halfway through his sentence.

Lara laughed shortly. "I'll keep that in mind," she cracked.

It still seemed incredible to Mindy that the woman she had seen on the screen in more than one supporting role was now being supportive of her. It was no secret that Lara Mancini had given up a promising movie career to follow her heart's dream of becoming a nurse.

If Lara could reinvent herself, Mindy thought, if she could walk away from budding fame and gobs of money to do something noble, then what she was trying to do with her own life should be a piece of cake.

After all, it wasn't as if she had walked away from an actual career. Despite her education and her degree in journalism, Brad hadn't wanted her to have a career. Her place was at his side while he forged his, he'd told her time and again. Because she loved him, she'd listened. And, she supposed, to his credit, there'd always been money to do whatever she wanted to do.

The trouble was, she always had to ask him for it. It embarrassed her, even though he had always dispensed it. Embarrassed her because she always had to tell him what she wanted the money for. At times, it felt like begging. She certainly never felt it was her money as well as his. He never lost an opportunity to drive the point home that he was the one who had earned the money, not her. When he gave it to her, he always jokingly referred to the money as her ''allowance.'' As if she were still a child in her parents' house.

Or worse, just a child. A child who was supposed to stand obediently by as her husband satisfied some inner craving and had affairs.

She clenched her hands on either side of her as she sat on the examination table.

''Is something wrong?'' Lara's soft voice broke into her thoughts.

Mindy shook off the morbid memories that threatened to overwhelm her. All that was behind her, she reminded herself. The best was yet to be. Right? She looked at Lara. ''No, why?''

''No reason. You just had a strange look on your face, that's all.'' Lara kept her voice cheerful. A cheerful disposition, Mindy had noticed, seemed to be a prerequisite for working at Manhattan Multiples, from the receptionist on up. ''If you have any questions, I'd be happy to sit down with you and answer them. Or just talk.'' Lara's eyes were kind. ''You're the last patient of the day.''

Mindy was touched. She had to stop feeling sorry for herself, she silently ordered. She was around people who genuinely cared about her and her babies. That was the important thing, not if she was going to turn into a whale for a few months.

"Thanks, but no. I was just thinking, that's all." She pressed her lips together. The intimate moment emboldened her. "Do you miss it?"

Lara tossed away the used paper from the table. "Miss what?"

Mindy looked to see if the doctor was listening, but he was still busy making notations in her chart. "Your career."

Lara smiled, as if this wasn't an original question. "*This* is my career."

Mindy didn't want to give offense, but she was curious. "I meant, do you miss making movies?"

Lara seemed to consider the question, then glanced at Derek, who watched her from hooded eyes. The two obviously were attracted to each other. "Do I miss standing around all day waiting to shoot two minutes of film that might or might not make it to the final cut? No, I like being active and there's always plenty of activity here." She grinned, sending another sidelong glance toward the doctor as he finished writing notes in Mindy's chart.

Derek flipped the chart closed and looked at Mindy. "So, we'll see you again in two weeks."

"I thought I was on a monthly schedule."

"That was just in the beginning," he told her. "Because you're carrying more than one baby, we want to be on top of things here, to make sure everything continues going smoothly for you. Besides, you can come here and complain to your heart's content." The support portion was the very heart of Manhattan

Multiples, and none of them ever lost sight of that. ‘‘Everyone will be very sympathetic to what you’re going through. Mothers of multiple babies have their own unique set of...um—’’ he hunted for the right word ‘‘—circumstances.’’

More like problems, Mindy thought. And she could readily identify with that. It was all she could do to place one foot in front of the other and deal with the path her life had taken.

Tempting though the thought was, and tempting though Lara’s invitation to stay and talk was, all she wanted to do tonight was fall into her own bed. The thought of sleep was more alluring than food was right now.

‘‘When will I stop being tired?’’ she wanted to know.

At the door the doctor looked at his watch, then back at her. ‘‘In about eighteen and a half years. If you’re lucky.’’ He glanced toward Lara. ‘‘Coming, Nurse?’’

Lara brightened slightly at the verbal byplay. ‘‘Right behind you, Doctor.’’

They had something going, Mindy thought. Or would very soon. The looks that went between the doctor and his nurse were too hot not to generate their own flame, if they hadn’t already.

Mindy couldn’t help the pang of envy that went through her.

Chapter Three

Eloise stood in the hallway before her office, directly in the path of foot traffic and lost in thought.

She'd had no luck yet with getting through to Bill Harper. His aides guarded him like those flying monkeys from *The Wizard of Oz.*

You'd think that the city of New York would help support an organization that dealt with pregnancies and specialized in multiple births.

Bill's betrayal still vexed her. How could he hold this grudge against her? And why couldn't he simply talk to her? It wasn't as if she was unapproachable, Eloise thought as she nodded at a couple of new members who hurried past her to the ladies' room. When she died, and if there was need for an autopsy, she was convinced that they would probably find one of the world's biggest hearts in her chest. She truly cared about what went on here and the people who were involved in Manhattan Multiples.

Caring was one of the reasons she'd started this center in the first place. She'd needed something into which she could channel her energy and her love. She needed something to fill the hole that had appeared when Walter was taken from her.

Even trying to lose herself in her sons' lives didn't take care of the problem for her. And as they became older, she knew Carl, Henry and John would have less and less need for her. They'd be going out into the world, testing their wings, forging paths for themselves. As well they should.

But that would leave her with increasingly less to do. She couldn't very well stay at home counting flowers on the wallpaper. So the idea for the center had been born, and she had taken the helm, dispensing the wisdom of her own experiences, seeking others to add to it, and all the while making a point of being in touch with every single woman who flew or waddled, depending on their state, through those doors.

A people person, she made herself accessible and hoped others would do the same for her.

So why was Bill shutting her out?

With a sigh Eloise shoved her hands into the pockets of her powder-blue skirt.

"You know, if you stand there long enough, someone is going to wind up walking into you.'' Allison Baker, her personal assistant, came up to her. ''Is anything wrong, Eloise?''

With a shake of her head, Eloise pulled herself out of her trance. For a second she was tempted to share her fears about Manhattan Multiples but then decided against it.

Damn, she wished she knew the answer.

Eloise realized that her prim-and-proper assistant was still waiting for an answer to her question. Eloise said the first thing that came to her mind, lame though it sounded. ''I'm just thinking, that's all.''

Allison nodded knowingly. ''About the mayor's proposed cutbacks?''

Allison was very intuitive and this shouldn't have been a surprise. Everyone on the Manhattan Multiples staff was talking about it, wondering if they should start updating their résumés and look for work. No one wanted that to happen. Working here was a joy, even at the worst of times.

''Yes.''

Allison hugged the thick binder she was holding a little closer to her chest. ''What do you plan to do?''

Eloise tossed her head. ''Fight this, of course.'' There'd never been any doubt in her mind that she would. Above all else, she'd been blessed with the courage of her own convictions. She would have thought that had become evident by now to everyone.

''I'm not one of those socialites who likes to sit back and watch her nail polish dry. Manhattan Multiples is a long way off from closing its doors. We have fund-raisers to throw and legal issues to stand on. If Bill Harper thinks that we're going to 'go gentle into that good night,' he definitely has another think coming.''

Twenty-something Josie Tate, Manhattan Multiples' very own walking, breathing tribute to the sixties hippie era as well as their head receptionist, turned the corner just in time to catch the last part of Eloise's declaration.

''Dylan Thomas, right?'' Josie asked brightly, guessing at the origin of Eloise's reference.

Glancing her way, Eloise nodded her reply. Josie was wearing a wide, ruffled skirt that contained every bright color known to civilized woman within its fabric. It was offset by a black velvet vest that seemed completely out of sync with the damp, humid July day outside the building. But then, Eloise had long since ceased being surprised by Josie's choice of clothing. And, in an odd sort of way, the twenty-five-year-old pseudo hippie/poet/receptionist added to the charm that was Manhattan Multiples just as much as the pastel decor and soothing music that was piped in during the day.

Self-taught and pleased with herself, Josie grinned. ''Hey, I wrote a new poem.'' She held up the piece of paper she'd labored over all last night. It was filled with handwriting only Josie could decipher. ''Anyone want to hear it?''

In her off hours, Josie wrote poetry and gave readings all over the city to receptive groups of budding poets and would-be musicians in search of lyrics. Her bright-blue eyes jumped from one woman to the other, as if eagerly waiting for a response.

"Only if it's something that would inspire a fight rally," Eloise told her.

Allison was already withdrawing. Although they were friends, they were as different in their approach to life and in their interests outside the center as night was to day. The expression on her heart-shaped face was apologetic. "Maybe later."

Undaunted, Josie pretended to sigh. "A prophet is never honored in her hometown."

"You hold that thought," Eloise advised with a laugh, patting her shoulder. "And in the meantime, see if you can come up with something catchy that we can use to help fry our illustrious mayor's butt."

"That seems like a waste," Josie confided. "The man's got one hell of a cute butt."

"Josie!" Allison looked at her friend incredulously. "He's the mayor."

"That doesn't stop him from having a cute butt—although the odds are against it." She grinned, turning toward Eloise. "I'll see what I can do," she promised.

Spinning on her heel, Josie headed back the way she'd come. Break was almost over and she had a desk to oversee and people to welcome.

* * *

It had been five days.

Jason flipped back the pages on his desk calendar. Time to stop trying to find fault with her, he decided. He pushed the calendar back on his desk. That was what he'd been doing, he thought. Consciously and unconsciously he'd been searching for flaws, for ways to get Mindy to give up and quit.

Who would have ever thought that he would one day be trying to push Mindy Conway away?

Mindy Richards, Jason reminded himself. She was Mindy Richards now, and with a husband in her life or not, she had no place in Jason's.

Nothing and no one had a place in his life except for work. He owed the people who paid him good money for advice 110 percent of his abilities—and the same portion of his mind. They weren't paying him to spend his time thinking about Mindy. Wondering about Mindy. Yearning for Mindy.

There, he'd said it, albeit silently. He wanted her. Wanted her in every sense of the word. That was no way for an employer to feel about someone who worked for him. That embodied the cornerstone of sexual harassment.

Except that he hadn't, of course. Hadn't touched her, hadn't harassed her. Had hardly said very much of anything that wasn't absolutely work related after that first day. The way he treated her, she might as well have been a stranger who had come in off the street.

Except that she wasn't.

Still, it was doing her a huge disservice to try to

fire her when she was so damn good, so damn eager. She actually looked as if she *liked* what she was doing. Nathalie was already saying that Mindy was invaluable and she didn't know how they'd gotten along without her all these years.

Nathalie *would* say that.

Having someone competent as an administrative assistant freed her up to enjoy her own life a little more. Not that Nathalie had conducted her life like a cloistered nun before Mindy had come on the scene. Twice married, and divorced just as many times, Nathalie knew how to kick up her heels and enjoy life to the fullest. None of the inhibitions that plagued normal men and women seemed to have been woven into her makeup.

That he behaved like a monk in a secluded mountainside monastery had always been a source of discontent for her. Nathalie acted as if getting him to come around was her own personal crusade. He was certain that the temps she'd hired before Mindy had all been chosen not for their office proficiency but for their looks. Each seemed to have been more pretty than the last. And all had been largely empty-headed.

Which brought him back full circle to Mindy.

Beauty and brains. It was a hard combination for a man to resist, and he found himself less and less inclined to do so with each day that went by. If it wasn't for the fact that he had a disastrous marriage in his background, he'd be sorely tempted to break self-imposed employer-employee regulations and ask Mindy out.

And ask for trouble along with it.

If it ain't broke, don't fix it, right?

And right now, Mindy Richards was the best thing that had ever happened to Mallory and Dixon since they had opened their doors. If he didn't want to scare her away, he knew he should just keep on going the way he had. Silently.

He had no business thinking what he was thinking. Had even less business getting up from his desk the way he was doing and proceeding to the outer office as if he was on automatic pilot.

Maybe he'd be lucky and she would have left for the day. For the weekend.

But he knew even before he set foot outside his own office that Mindy was still sitting at her desk. For one, she never left without saying good-night, her very words ensuring that at least it would be, as long as he could continue replaying the sound of her voice uttering them in his head.

For another, there was her perfume. It was still as gut-stirringly present as ever. He wondered if there was some way he could get her to stop wearing it so that it would stop haunting him.

He was right. She was there, in the process of powering down her computer and getting her things together. For a second he just stood and watched her. Why did every movement she made seem like poetry?

This was no way for a grown man to think, he told himself.

It didn't stop him.

He had to say something before she turned around to see him staring at her. He didn't want her to think he was stalking her. Even if they did belong in the same office at the same time.

Not wanting to startle her, Jason cleared his throat. "Getting ready to go home?"

He could see by the way she jumped that he'd startled her, anyway.

His deep voice shimmered along her skin, melting into her consciousness. Mindy swung around in her chair to look at him.

Jason hadn't talked to her very much these past four days. Just small sound bites aimed at whatever detail he wanted her to see to. And then he'd been gone, lingering like smoke in her mind but not in fact.

She half thought she imagined the sound of his voice now, but there he was, in his doorway. The next moment he was walking toward her.

Mindy nodded toward the clock on the wall. "It's after five. I thought I'd close up shop." Nathalie had already left for what she'd announced was going to be a very long, very sexy weekend, hinting that she probably was going to spend most of it in bed. The vibrant woman had punctuated the last remark with a significant look aimed at Jason that neither he, nor she, had missed.

Her purse hovered over the drawer as she held it aloft. ''Unless you need me for something.''

He couldn't help it. The remark made him laugh. If she only knew, he thought.

Jason saw a wide smile crease her lips in response. ''I forgot you could do that.''

He wasn't following her. ''Do what?''

''Laugh. Not that I heard you do it very often in high school,'' she confessed. The times that she had, it had sent warm ripples through her stomach. It was the kind of deep, sexy laugh that pulled you in, painting improbable, unattainable scenarios in your head.

Surprised, Jason leaned a hip against her desk as he folded his arms before his chest. He probed a little. ''I didn't think that you were even aware of me in high school.''

''I asked you to sign my yearbook,'' Mindy reminded him.

That had made an impression on him, but one that he'd thought was fueled only by his own imagination. He'd never possessed a bloated ego. ''I thought you were asking everyone.''

She looked at him for a second. Was he serious? Didn't he know how many girls would have loved to have gone out with him? That he'd been the school's brooding man of mystery? They'd all held their breaths to see who he'd ask to the prom. And when he didn't ask anyone, or attend, they'd all thought that was so typically Jason, to be above mundane things like proms and graduation parties.

"There was hardly room in my book for everyone. Just the people I wanted." God, did that sound as much of a come-on as she thought it did? She sincerely hoped the blush she felt forming inside her wouldn't rise up to color her face.

He lifted a shoulder, letting it drop. She was just being polite, nothing more.

"Our paths didn't exactly cross." She'd been part of every major event that took place in high school, while Jason had simply kept to himself, his focus on his goals. Only, his mind had remained on her.

Maybe he didn't remember, she thought. Maybe she'd only imagined that he'd look her way. Maybe it was someone else who had caught his attention and she'd only been in his line of sight, as invisible as air to him. Still, her pride made her remind him. "You were in my math class. And in economics."

He was really surprised that she'd even noticed that, much less remembered it. He truly doubted that she was aware of the fact that he used to come in early just to watch her walk through the door. And wish he were one of the guys who clustered around her.

But it wasn't in his nature to cluster, and the risks he took were never truly risks, but completely calculated actions. Putting himself out there, exposed, was not the way he operated.

"Really? I don't remember."

To say that she did, that she even remembered some of the outfits he wore, like that black turtleneck sweater he seemed to favor and those tight jeans that had caused her to actually snap her pencil in two the first day she'd seen him walking into class wearing them, would have placed her in an awkward position.

So instead, to save face, something that she had very little of these days, Mindy merely shrugged her slim shoulders. "You were kind of hard to miss." In case he got the wrong idea, she quickly added, "You sat in front of Terry Malone."

Terry Malone. Tall, blond. Rich. Perfect. With three track-and-field letters adorning his school jacket. Had he been able to find a picture of the guy, Terry's face would have adorned the dartboard on the back of his bedroom door.

"Right. Your boyfriend."

Mindy looked at him sharply. Jason couldn't have known that, if he'd been as unaware of her as he was leading her to believe.

A little ripple of satisfaction danced through her.

She smiled. "It all seems like such a very long time ago."

"Yeah, well—"

Straightening, Jason looked toward the outer office door. He should be going. Now. Before he said something stupid and had to have his foot surgically removed from his mouth.

He was going to leave, Mindy thought. To go to whatever life he had outside of this office. Her evening and the weekend that was to follow was going to be spent trying to make the tiny one-room apartment she rented into a home.

Suddenly she didn't feel like going there, didn't feel like being alone.

She could always go to Manhattan Multiples, she supposed. There was always someone there to talk to, even as late as ten o'clock. She could even take Lara Mancini up on her offer, if the woman was there tonight.

Or she could go to see her parents. That was always a viable option. Her parents always made her feel welcome and wanted.

But she didn't want to be someone's patient or someone's daughter tonight. She wanted to feel the way she used to, like someone who could have the world at her feet if she just applied herself.

Like someone whose husband hadn't run her self-esteem into the ground and cheated on her. Like someone whose husband hadn't said, "that's tough," when she'd told him she was pregnant.

She wanted the bright, shining life she thought she had when she'd graduated high school.

Without realizing it, Mindy allowed a sigh to escape her lips.

She might not have realized it, but Jason did. He heard her. It stopped him in his tracks and made him turn from the door. And say something he had absolutely no intention of saying.

"Would you like to go somewhere and get a cup of coffee?"

He watched Mindy brighten like a thirsty flower turning up its head toward the first spring rain. "I'd love to."

Big mistake.

The warning echoed in his head. But the sound of her response drowned it out. So he smiled, ignoring the former, replaying the latter, and said, "Then let's go. Places around here tend to fill up fast with people escaping to the first leg of their weekend."

Purse in hand, she was on her feet instantly. "Let's," she agreed.

Chapter Four

Sitting outside at a table for two at a nearby trendy restaurant, Jason solemnly watched the late-afternoon sun making shimmering patterns on the surface of his coffee.

The noise of the city pushed its way in, surrounding him and Mindy. The silence that existed between them was all he was aware of.

He had to admit that he hadn't thought this out.

Being moved exclusively by the desire for Mindy's company, he'd forgotten that in order to share it comfortably, he was going to have to talk with her.

Talking, when it didn't involve the care and feeding of investment funds, was not his long suit. It never had been. He had never been accused of being one of those people blessed with a golden tongue. Not even fool's gold. And right now, his tongue felt as if it had been forged out of two tons of lead.

''So,'' was all he could manage before he had utterly depleted his supply of words. It sank to the bottom of his cup of coffee like a stone.

Mindy smiled at him, looking over the rim of her recently stirred cup of foam and decaf, her eyes stirring him.

''So,'' she echoed, waiting for him to make some kind of stab at conversation.

Well, that had gone nowhere, he thought darkly. When in doubt, ask questions. That way the spotlight was focused somewhere other than on him.

He took a sip of the strong, black cup of unaffected coffee, let it wind its hot, dark path down his throat and through his chest, then ventured forward. ''Care to fill in the blanks?''

She tilted her head in that way he'd always thought hopelessly endearing. ''Excuse me?''

He was going to have to stop talking in bits and pieces, he thought, and make sense before she thought he was hopelessly sentence challenged.

''The blanks between walking on stage to get your diploma and arriving at Mallory and Dixon on Monday morning.'' He did a quick subtraction. ''That leaves us with what, eleven years?''

Eleven years. The simple statement stunned her. My God, was it really all that time? Had that many years actually gone by since she'd left for Northwestern, determined to set the world on fire?

It didn't seem possible.

She felt as if the distance between then and now was a little more than a blink of an eye. A year, maybe two, no more than three. Eleven? How had that happened?

"Eleven years," she echoed out loud. Her mouth curved in a self-deprecating smile. "That suddenly makes me feel very old."

He hadn't meant to do that. "Someone once said everyone has to grow older, but you don't have to grow old."

She recalled reading that someplace. Mindy thought for a second, then her eyes brightened as she remembered. "George Burns, I think."

He was surprised that she knew something like that. But then, she'd been surprising him all week. He took another sip of coffee, wishing there was something in the drink that would transform his stilted tongue into a glib one. He began to understand what had driven Christian to approach Cyrano and ask the character to do his talking for him.

"Good words to live by." He allowed himself to study her face for a moment. He'd noticed women looking in her direction enviously as they walked by. "In any case, I don't think you have anything to worry about in that department for a very long, long time."

She raised her eyes to his, and for one moment he forgot to breathe.

"That's very sweet of you."

Embarrassed, not knowing what to do with his face, his eyes, his hands, Jason shrugged. "Just stating a fact."

Sweet. Who would have ever thought that Jason Mallory could actually be described that way? Mindy mused. Tough, rugged, sexy, yes, but sweet? That was a new one.

She sat back, enjoying this lovely island of time that had materialized out of nowhere, not unaware of the envious looks she was garnering. She would bet that every woman who walked by wished that she was in her place.

The conversation had stopped again. Searching for something to move it along, Jason looked down at her hand. He heard himself asking another personal question before he had a chance to think it out. "So, are you divorced, or—?"

"Or," she replied. It was a state of limbo, really, not quite married anymore, not yet divorced. "It's not final yet." Anyday now, she thought.

The sun was pushing its way into the restaurant, brushing against the wide gold band, highlighting it. "Oh, I was just wondering because you're still wearing your wedding ring."

Mindy looked down at the gold band as if it had somehow managed to offend her through no fault of its own. She wasn't wearing the ring because of any real sentimental attachment. The truth was, the only part of her that had gained weight since she'd become pregnant was her hands. Actually, not even her hands, just her hand. Her left one.

The fingers of her left hand had swollen just enough to make easy removal of her wedding ring an impossibility. Tugging at it was futile. Like a guest who had intentionally overstayed their welcome, the ring refused to be dislodged. The only way to rid herself of it was to cut it off, and she really wasn't ready to do that at the moment.

Somehow that would have underscored the mistake she'd made in giving her heart to Brad and putting her life on virtual hold. Cutting the ring off would have symbolized her making a complete break with that part of her life, and though she was struggling to be independent now, she wasn't ready to bury everything just yet. But soon, very soon, she promised herself. And then she was going to have to send it back to Brad.

But she didn't want to tell Jason any of this.

She thought of a movie she'd once seen. The heroine pretended to be married in order not to have anyone hit on her.

Mindy ran her thumb over the row of winking diamonds slowly. "Oh that. I just wear it to keep the wolves away."

He felt a sense of relief and told himself he shouldn't. "I thought that you were still wearing it because you and your husband were trying to reconcile.''

The very idea threatened to make Mindy gag. ''Never happen,'' she told him flatly. She set the cup down a little too hard and some of the liquid sloshed over the side. She moved her napkin over to sop up the mess. If only the mess that her life had become was as easily cleaned up, she thought. ''I've always disliked having to take a number and wait in line, like in a bakery or at the post office.''

His eyes narrowed as he tried to fathom what the remark had to do with the state of her marriage. ''I don't understand—''

''Neither did I. Glossed right over the evidence, even though it was right there in front of me.'' The excuses, the late nights, the faint scent of perfume that wasn't hers, the hang-up calls when she answered the phone. ''Believed every word he said when he told me he was working late.'' She looked at him. Did he think her a hopeless fool to be so naive? ''People do work late in this day and age.''

''But he wasn't working.'' It wasn't a question, it was rhetorical. And hit so close to home that he couldn't believe it. Debra had played the same game with him, lying to him when she bothered saying anything at all to him.

She laughed shortly. ''Oh, he was working all right.'' Holding up her hand, she enumerated, counting the women off on her fingers one by one. ''Working over his secretary, his assistant, some of his prettier clients. I always thought that Brad's main problem was that he spread himself around too much.'' She shook her head. Sometimes, it was hard even for her to believe how blind she'd been, how trusting. ''I had no idea how right I was. It was like he spread himself and his seed all over the state of Illinois.'' Mindy looked down at her hands. She'd knotted them together in her lap. ''I guess I just wasn't woman enough to keep him at home or satisfied.''

He felt a flash of anger rising within him. Anger at the man who had done this to her, anger at the sheer absurdity of what she was suggesting. Didn't she see what she had to offer a man?

''Seems to me the problem's with him, not you.'' She looked at him, confusion knitting in her brow. ''Any man who goes from woman to woman is looking to bolster a very sagging self-esteem and has severe psychological deficiencies. He needs validation. None of that has anything to do with you.''

Jason was being very kind, but that still didn't erase what she was feeling. Brad's shabby treatment of her had made her doubt herself in the most severe way. ''I don't know about that.''

''I do. Otherwise, your husband—'' He knew she'd referred to him by name, but right now he was drawing a blank. ''What did you say his name was?''

''Brad.''

''Brad.'' He'd never liked that name, Jason thought. It sounded as if it belonged to some shallow narcissistic preppy. ''Brad would have been more than happy to stay at home and count himself lucky to have a woman like you for his wife.''

He had completely overwhelmed her. Warmth enveloped her, easing away the cold lump of self-doubt. ''Wow. I don't know what to say.''

He hadn't said that to get any kind of response. ''The truth doesn't need to be commented on. It just exists.'' Jason looked over toward their waiter. The man was unsubtly hovering, eyeing their small table. In the not-too-far distance, separated by a rope, were would-be patrons all waiting to be seated. Jason nodded toward her empty cup. ''Would you like to order anything else?''

''No, this was fine,'' she told him, pushing back her coffee cup.

In deference to her condition, she had ordered decaf, but even so, she knew that the drink would go straight through her. Mentally, Mindy ticked off forty-five minutes from her first sip, knowing that was approximately all the time she'd have before her first bathroom run. If she had any more coffee, that would just speed up her relays.

Jason shifted forward, taking his wallet out of his pocket. He pulled out a twenty and placed it on the table. ''Then I think we're going to have to leave. The crowd looks like it could get ugly.''

Rising to his feet, he took her arm. He escorted her out, maneuvering through the throng and not saying anything until they reached the entrance. The scent of her hair seemed to swirl around him as he pushed open the door for her and followed her out. He could feel his gut tightening in response.

Hungry, he was hungry, he thought. That was the problem. Nothing a little steak dinner couldn't cure.

As if.

The second they walked out the door, the oppressive heat hit them. It was all Mindy could do to keep from wilting. It was like walking into an oven set at five hundred degrees. She felt as if her eyelashes were in danger of melting.

Jason felt her sag a little against him. His hand tightened on her arm. ''Something wrong?''

Mindy shook her head, rallying. For a second, there, the change in temperature from the restaurant to the street had her knees feeling rubbery.

Or was it just a by-product of being pregnant, she wondered.

She hung on to his arm for support. ''No, I just forgot how humid summers in New York could be. I feel as if someone just lobbed a fireball in my direction.''

Now that he looked at her, she did look a little pale. ''There's air-conditioning in my car. Can I drop you somewhere?''

The bus she took stopped just across the street. There was already a long line. His offer was tempting. Still, she couldn't just put him out like that. ''Oh, no, I don't want to be a bother.''

She *wasn't* a bother. The thoughts he was having

about her, the desire that kept skewering him at unexpected times, *that* was a bother, but not her.

"I told you before, I don't say anything I don't mean. If I thought that dropping you off somewhere would be a bother, I wouldn't have offered." How many times did he have to make that clear to her? "Shall we take it from the top?"

"Well, I don't live too far from here if you take it as the crow flies." She bit her lip, looking at the clogged streets. Driving her home would be an ordeal this time of day. "But if the crow's driving a car and stuck in traffic..."

He laughed at the image. There was no doubt about it; being around her made him feel good. Too good. He had to be careful.

"You'll make the same time in a bus," he pointed out. "And at least in my car, you don't run the risk of having to stand next to someone who had garlic bread with his lunch."

He definitely had a point. Mindy felt herself losing more ground. She was trying to do the right thing, but her condition made his offer exceptionally tempting. Besides, she really did like being in his company, even if she had to do most of the talking.

She smiled at him. "You do put up a persuasive argument when you want to."

It was as if someone else was doing the talking for him. He heard himself say, "I only want to when the stakes are right."

Taking her arm again, he guided her to the curb,

keeping his body between her and at least one branch of strident pedestrians.

Mindy was grateful for the buffer. She'd forgotten how aggressive New Yorkers could be. And how plentiful. Living in the suburbs the way she had ever since she'd married Brad, she'd become accustomed to having plenty of elbow room. On the streets of New York, especially during certain hours, there was no such thing as elbow room. Even grounded chickens would have found themselves hard-pressed to flap their wings without hitting something.

It took longer to walk the three blocks back to the building where Jason's office was located than it had to reach the restaurant in the first place. People kept coming at them like a steady stream of bullets. She started to feel just the slightest bit light-headed again and hung on to Jason's arm. And then suddenly she wasn't moving at all.

Looking down, Mindy saw that the heel of her shoe had gotten caught in the subway grating. "Wait," she cried out. "I'm stuck."

Without a word, Jason took in the situation, then dropped to one knee beside her. With one hand on her ankle and one bracing the back of her shoe, he worked her heel out of the grating. Mindy felt a trail of heat travel swiftly up her leg even after he'd removed his hand from her ankle. She felt a little like a modern-day Cinderella. If Cinderella had had to flee from the castle over subway grating.

"I guess chivalry isn't dead," Mindy commented as Jason took her arm again.

No one had ever accused him of that before. He shrugged off the comment. "It was either get your shoe out of the grating or carry you," he told her gruffly.

Entering the office building, they took the elevator down to the parking garage nestled in its bowels. At this time of the evening, it was a hub of activity as car after car queued up to leave its darkened lair in order to hit the hot streets and head for a little mindless entertainment, or just home. Anywhere but where it had just spent the last soul-dampening eight hours.

His silver Morgan was parked on the first level. Even so, it looked as if they were going to have a long wait before they got out of the building again.

"This might take a while," he warned as he let her in on the passenger side.

Maybe Mindy would have been better off waiting for her bus, he thought, glancing at her as he slowly backed out of his space.

The plush leather upholstery sighed softly as she secured her seat belt around her. The English vehicle had to be the last word in luxury, she thought. Jason certainly had done well for himself. Though she had absolutely nothing to do with it, she couldn't help feeling rather proud of him.

"That's all right, I'm not in any hurry to get home."

It occurred to him that he hadn't asked for her address. "Where is home?" he asked, then added as they inched along toward the front booth and relative freedom. "Not that we're about to get there anytime soon."

He pressed down on the brake as they came to yet another stop. There were definitely times when he felt that walking was the fastest way of getting around in Manhattan. Gridlock here was pretty much a fact of life these days.

She gave him the address. It wasn't really that far away, but in this blistering, damp heat, the distance would have seemed almost insurmountable if she'd had to walk it. Reaching over, he switched on the air-conditioning, flipping the switch on high.

Mindy looked at him uncertainly. "Shouldn't we wait until the car is actually moving more than one inch an hour? You might ruin the engine."

He was struck by her thoughtfulness. A lot of other people in her position would have only thought of their own comfort, not the cost to the car. Her husband must have been an A-number-one jerk to have stepped out on her like that. Some men never knew when they had it good.

"Don't worry about it. That's one of the perks of owning a high-price luxury car. Aside from having mechanics charge you an arm and a leg whenever you drive in for an oil change or a tune-up, the air-conditioning units are strong enough to actually make a difference no matter what speed you're traveling."

He suppressed a sigh as they were forced to stop again. "Or not traveling, as the case may be."

The cool air coming out of the vents bathed her face and neck, and she began to feel human once more. She hadn't realized she'd shut her eyes until she was opening them again. They were finally emerging from the subterranean cave.

She shifted toward Jason. God, but his profile looked almost chiseled out of rock. "Are you sure I'm not keeping you from anything, am I?"

Once on the street, sunshine hit his face full force, creating a halo of light around him. Making him seem more godlike than he already was. If she didn't move her tongue, it was going to be permanently paralyzed any second.

Mindy held up her hands to forestall another protest. "I know, I know, you wouldn't have said it if you didn't mean it."

Jason allowed the tiniest of smiles to work the corners of his mouth. "You do catch on fast."

That was a laugh. "Not as fast at times as I should have." She shifted forward in her seat. The air-conditioning was doing a great deal to soothe her agitation. She began to relax a little. "Otherwise, I would have recognized Brad for what he was and not wasted all those years on him."

He'd never finished asking her his question in the restaurant. Stopping at the first light, he glanced at her. "What happened to your career?"

"What career?"

"The one you were supposed to have after you graduated." He knew she'd gone to Northwestern as a journalist major and fully expected to one day turn on the television and see her face looking back at him. He'd counted on it.

"Oh, that career." It would have been easy to give in to self-pity. Easy, but not very productive, and she was a firm believer in always looking forward. There was nothing she could do about the past, except to learn from it. "I met Brad in my senior year, fell in love, and everything else paled in comparison. When he asked me to stay in Illinois and be his wife, nothing else mattered. And when he asked that I be supportive of his career, put my energies into helping him establish himself, I didn't think anything of it. Didn't feel resentful," she tagged on in a whisper.

"But now you do."

Having noble goals was one thing, but she wasn't about to lie. "Damn right I do."

They were moving again. At the speed of a drowsy snail. "So why didn't you do something about it when you left him?"

"Do something?" She didn't understand what he was driving at.

"Why didn't you follow your dream?" To have landed a job as an administrative assistant for a securities firm was light-years away from being a journalist, no matter how helpful she was becoming to them.

"Nobody would hire me without experience, and I

had to eat.'' She stared straight ahead. Providing for herself and her future babies was all that mattered. Dreams were for people without responsibilities. ''Maybe someday,'' she whispered quietly.

But he heard her and took it to mean that she was back in his life only temporarily. But then, he already knew that.

Chapter Five

"This is where you live?"

He didn't mean it to sound the way it did, as if he was being critical of her home. But while her address was still in a good neighborhood, it just barely squeaked through. There was no doorman, from what he could see. Far from as a status symbol, he thought of a doorman in terms of protection for her. And she didn't seem to have one.

He lived in a three-bedroom apartment in SoHo that he rattled around in without being able to find a place for himself. Maybe they should trade, he thought wryly.

Mindy nodded in response to his question. Moving into a studio apartment after living in a two-story, five-bedroom house took some adjustment, but it was all part of reinventing herself. Of finding her inner stamina and tapping into it, not for herself but for the babies who were to be. It had certainly put a premium on priorities for her. She had to be very selective when it came to what she used to decorate her new home.

Mindy shifted a little in her seat, preparing to get out of the vehicle. She knew Jason couldn't double park for more than a couple of seconds. "It's not much, but I call it home."

He glanced out of the window up to the dark-brown twelve-story building. He noted that there were air-conditioning units hanging out of some of the windows. That meant no central air. It appeared to be one of the older buildings in the vicinity.

"Which apartment's yours?" he wanted to know.

"I've got a studio apartment on the third floor."

"A studio?" He looked up toward where she'd pointed. The window was barren. No air conditioner. She had to be sweltering in this kind of weather.

"It's all I need," Mindy told him quickly.

At least, she thought, it was all she needed for the time being, until the babies came. Then it was going to definitely be crammed. But the small studio was all she could afford on her own. Refusing the money that both her mother and her father had tried to slip her at separate times hadn't been easy, but she'd done it and was proud of herself.

She kept reminding herself of that feeling whenever she started to feel claustrophobic within her apartment's limited space.

But now that she had a job, she could afford to get a better, bigger place by the time the babies arrived. She hoped. It wasn't exactly as if apartments in the city grew on trees and were easy to come by or affordable when they did crop up. The standing joke about people keeping an eye out on the obituary page was not as far-fetched as it sounded. Places were almost that hard to find.

Nope, Jason decided, the building gave no indication that thoughts of a doorman had even remotely crossed the builder's mind when it was conceived.

Summer hours being what they were, it was hardly dark, but there were rules he liked to follow. "Maybe I'd better walk you to your door."

A tiny jab of panic pierced her. She didn't want him seeing just how small her apartment really was. Studio apartments varied in sizes, and hers had to be the first size up from being labeled a closet.

She pointed toward the street ahead. "No, that's all right. You can't exactly put your car in your pocket, and there's no place to park."

But even as she said it, an early-model Cadillac was painfully angling itself out of a space three spots down the block.

He slanted a glance toward her. "I guess luck's with us."

"I guess," she murmured, sliding down just a hair in her seat.

As often as she'd daydreamed about Jason Mallory walking her to her door after spending an evening with her, she didn't want it to become a reality. He was ever-so-obviously well-off. In the week she'd been there, she'd been placed in charge of their books and had gotten a rough idea of how much the firm was worth. It had been a long time since she'd seen so many digits lodged together in one place.

While she, on the other hand, had exactly seventeen dollars in her wallet, fifty in her checking account and whatever was due her after taxes for the week she'd put in. Everything else, because of the pending divorce, was in limbo.

The Prince and the Pauper with a new spin, she thought.

As she sneaked a look at Jason's profile, it suddenly occurred to her that she didn't even know his marital status. He hadn't volunteered it, and Nathalie hadn't mentioned anything about Jason's current personal situation, although the older woman had been very free with details about her own life.

The last thing she wanted was for a Mrs. Mallory to think of her as some kind of competition who was trying to bed her husband.

Mindy started opening the passenger door even before he finished parking. ''It's all right, really,'' she said.

''I'd feel better.''

His tone told her that he wasn't about to be argued out of this.

Carefully he eased his car into the recently vacated spot, beating out an SUV that became aware of the space just half a block too late. He did it with the ease of someone who was accustomed to maneuvering in tight spaces.

Getting out, Jason had barely enough room to make it around the hood of his Morgan to the curb. He opened her door for her and took her hand just as she began to climb out.

Their eyes met and held for a moment. Behind her, she heard the owner of the SUV shout some choice words before continuing his search for a parking place. But her attention was focused on Jason, on the feel of his fingers locked securely around her hand. On the strange way he made her feel.

"I don't remember you being this chivalrous in high school."

He shut the passenger door, then aimed his key ring at it. The quick squeak that came in response told him his security system was engaged. "I doubt if you remember anything at all about me in high school."

"Then you'd lose that bet," she informed him, walking ahead to the building's outer door.

He watched her for a second, allowing the tempting sway of her hips to seep into his consciousness. Then he increased his stride and made it to the front entry door first. He opened it for her.

Her response had him wondering, but there was no polite way to find out exactly what she meant by it.

They weren't in that kind of place in their relationship. He doubted if they ever would be.

Had she even thought about him back then? Were there missed opportunities he'd known nothing about?

Probably not.

Walking into the small foyer that smelled of damp, recently washed floors, Mindy glanced toward the elevator, located directly opposite the block of mailboxes. She didn't bother with the latter. No one knew she was here yet, so there'd be no mail for her other than the few pieces marked Occupant. They could keep.

The sign taped over one of the elevator doors proclaimed it to be out of order. Again. Since she'd moved in less than a month ago, the elevator had been functional exactly twelve days out of twenty-nine. It wasn't a good omen.

"Looks like Mr. Oshinsky is going to have to get busy again," she commented.

"Mr. Oshinsky?" Jason echoed.

"The superintendent."

Jason frowned at the darkened door. "This happen often?"

She had no way of knowing that, only hoped that it didn't. "It's been a bad month," she replied vaguely.

That didn't have a good ring to it. He didn't like thinking of Mindy living here, but there was absolutely nothing he could do about it. He had no say in her life, other than as her boss. His authority didn't cross over into this realm. ‘‘Maybe he needs a better manual on how to fix elevators.’’

She grinned, and he felt a little sunshine spreading out in the dimly lit foyer. ‘‘Maybe. Well—’’ she put her hand out to shake his ‘‘—thank you for the coffee. I’ll see you on Monday.’’

He looked at her hand and refrained from taking it. ‘‘Do you live in the foyer?’’

‘‘No.’’ Feeling slightly awkward, she dropped her hand to her side. ‘‘Why?’’

‘‘I said I’d walk you to your door,’’ Jason reminded her.

‘‘It’s two flights up,’’ she protested.

Was there some reason she didn’t want him coming up? Was there someone waiting for her? The smart thing would have been just to withdraw.

But he’d used up his quota of smarts for the day. ‘‘Mindy, investment counselors are supposed to be able to count. I know how many flights it takes to reach a third-floor apartment.’’

‘‘It’s hot and there’s no air-conditioning in the halls.’’ Or currently in her apartment, but she didn’t want him to know that.

He pretended to look around. ‘‘I noticed that.’’ And then his eyes came to rest on her. ‘‘I’ve also occasionally been known to be observant.’’

Eleven years ago this would have thrilled her. But not now. ‘‘Then you’re going to walk me upstairs?’’

‘‘That’s the plan.’’

She had a feeling that the more she protested, the

more Jason would dig in. Might as well get it over with. ''Okay.''

She led the way to the stairwell.

There didn't seem to be any air in the enclosed area. Certainly none she could feel. Perspiration had formed a small continuous line down her spine before she even reached the top of the third landing.

Mercifully Jason pushed the door open for her. She wasn't feeling all that strong right now. These babies, though tiny, seemed to be sapping all her strength these days. At the least opportune times.

''This is it,'' she announced as she came to the front of 3C. ''You've accomplished your mission, Captain, and seen me to my door.'' She unlocked her door and turned the knob, pushing the door partially open.

Turning back to him, for one wild, unguarded moment, she debated extending an invitation. Wondering if it was wise.

He glanced in. The interior looked cheery. And small. Incredibly small. He'd seen bigger closets in the last apartment he and Debra had considered before they'd taken the one where he was presently living.

Mindy looked up at him. There was no one else on the floor at the moment, and even the noise from the streets seemed to have faded away. How many times had she pictured something like this, Jason standing with her before her door, their very breaths touching?

Grow up, Mindy. Those daydreams belong to a teenager, not to a mother-to-be.

There was a line of perspiration just forming along his brow. It took everything she had not to feather her fingers across it to wipe the line away.

Against her better judgment, she began to entertain ideas that had no place in this situation. No place in her life, really.

Warm feelings moved across her like white cotton clouds across a blue sky. Crowding her.

Desperate, she reached for a deterrent, something to stop her in her tracks. ''Are you married…or anything?''

''Not even anything.''

The words fell from his lips as slowly as if they were encased in molasses and this was Vermont in January. He had a very real, very strong urge to kiss her. The heat was making him lose what little good sense he still possessed.

She pressed her lips together. ''Would you like to come in for some water?''

Water would be nice. She would be better.

Which was why he couldn't take her up on her invitation. He really wasn't thinking all that clearly this evening. If he had been, he would have remained with his car downstairs and would have been driving home right now.

''I'd better go,'' he told her.

By all rights he knew he should be backing away. But his feet remained exactly where they'd been on the checkered linoleum, as if glued there by the fresh layer of floor wax.

Don't go. "You probably have a full weekend planned," Mindy murmured, tilting her head up to his.

"Absolutely full," he agreed. He couldn't take his eyes off her face. He memorized every contour, every nuance. If need be, he could have recreated it in clay with his eyes shut. "Bursting at the seams." His voice felt as if it was some disembodied entity, echoing in some far-off place.

He slipped his hand along her cheek, his fingers straying into her soft hair, getting lost there. Just as lost as he was in her eyes.

Trying not to think at all because thinking would only make him back away, Jason inclined his head and brought his mouth down to hers.

The sweetness instantly overwhelmed him.

It was just as he'd imagined it. And so much better.

So much more.

But he wasn't prepared for the passion. That was a surprise.

Drawing her closer to him, his hands left her hair and traveled down the length of her, holding her to him. Embracing her, as the kiss, born of need and curiosity, deepened until it encompassed the entire world as he knew it.

Nothing was ever going to be the same again.

Mindy let herself go. She didn't think that she was kissing her boss, or that she was three months pregnant with what promised to be very demanding twins. She didn't think of the wedding ring that was on her finger, a symbol of something she hadn't until this very moment been prepared to completely relinquish.

She didn't think at all; she only felt.

Felt as if she was on fire.

Felt wonderful.

Cleaving to Jason, her body trembling within, she kissed him back. Kissed him hard and with all the longing that had populated her days and haunted her nights as she'd stayed up, waiting for the husband who never seemed to come home anymore.

Brad and his infidelities had done a number on her, had made her feel ugly and unattractive. Someone he turned to if there was nothing better available. He'd made her doubt herself to the point that just before she'd left she didn't know who or what she was.

But Jason was kissing her as if his very existence depended on it. As if he wanted and desired her above anything else. Whether it was true or not, she didn't know. What she did know was that she needed this, needed the validation he was unwittingly offering her. Needed him.

She was always going to be grateful to him for this. For making her feel, in one rousing, exhilarating moment, that she was all woman.

And then they were parting. And she found herself looking up at him, a little stunned and a lot dazed. And very happy.

What the hell had he just allowed himself to do?

Damn it all, was he crazy? Jason upbraided himself. At the very least this could be seen as sexually harassing her. And at the most…

At the most, he was traveling down roads he'd promised himself he wouldn't travel down again. Ever. He hadn't the right.

Shaken, he blew out a breath as he ran his hand through his dark hair.

Apologies didn't seem like nearly enough. But they were all he had. He hoped she didn't misunderstand. "I'm sorry."

Mindy's eyes widened as she looked up at him. The apology stung the second it was out.

Did he think she wanted an apology?

Was he just paying lip service, or did he actually regret what he'd just done?

Why?

Why would he regret it when she so clearly hadn't? When she'd given him no indication that he'd stepped over some line she didn't want him to cross?

Mindy swallowed before she risked saying anything, afraid that she might squeak like a mouse that had just run a long-distance marathon.

"I'm not." With that, she decided it was better to withdraw before he could say anything else, like, "Maybe you'd better find another job."

Jason wanted to make amends, to apologize. He didn't make a practice of this kind of thing. Since Debra, he hadn't even kissed another woman, despite Nathalie's numerous attempts to set him up. "I don't know what came over me."

The next thing he was going to say was that he was acting crazy. She didn't want to hear it. She wanted to go into her apartment and savor the taste of his lips on hers. And pretend, just for a little while, that she was absolutely carefree and on the cusp of the best romance of her life. She needed this as much as she needed a job, as much as she needed the air she breathed.

Any further apologies from Jason would crack the misty walls around her.

She swung open her door all the way. ''Must have been the lack of oxygen coming up the stairs,'' she cracked. ''The air's pretty thick up here. Thanks for the coffee. See you Monday.''

With that, Mindy closed the door behind her.

He stood staring at it for a long moment, debating whether to knock and ask to come in.

To apologize?

To make love with her?

He wasn't sure which. One he didn't really mean, one he'd regret. It was best if he said nothing, did nothing, just went home.

So he turned on his heel and walked toward the stairwell.

Until right this moment he would have said that his world was as upended as it was ever going to be.

Showed that you just never knew. Not even about yourself.

As he opened the door to the stairwell, he heard

the sound of a chain being slipped into its space and a lock being flipped.

He spent the weekend working to avoid playing mental Ping-Pong with himself. Dwelling on what had happened on Friday wasn't going to change anything.

People kissed all the time. Under the right set of circumstances he would have kissed her eleven years ago. Those circumstances just hadn't come up, he thought, getting himself what had to have been his twelfth cup of coffee of the morning.

He didn't have time to waste yearning for what might have been. Nor did he have time to concern himself with the fact that kissing Mindy might very well have been one of the stupidest things he had ever done.

Because kissing her had only made him want more, and there couldn't be more.

Even if there wasn't that prickly issue of her working for him, after what had happened with Debra, he knew he wasn't exactly well versed in relationships. Venturing out on a limb and attempting another go at a relationship that could result in disaster just wasn't what he needed right now.

Or ever.

Nothing ventured might mean nothing gained, but it also meant nothing lost, either.

Besides, the stock market was hiccuping all over the place. The phones at the office had been ringing off the hook all week with calls coming in from his clients, begging for direction and assurance. They were his first concern, not his stillborn love life.

He'd worked all through Saturday and kept the midnight oil burning as he stayed up with the latest reports his investment interns had generated. And only occasionally, as he got up to get something to eat within the spacious, throbbingly empty SoHo apartment that he had shared with Debra, did his thoughts turn to a woman with laughing eyes and lips that tasted like ripe strawberries.

Sunday he'd run on coffee and coffee fumes, working for as long as he could. Sunday his resolve crumbled a little more.

The temperature, according to the man on the radio beside his desk, was rising at a prodigious rate. Unwanted records were going to be smashed. New York City was in danger of becoming deep fried.

Though he did his best to block them out, thoughts of Mindy in her small apartment kept assaulting his brain. The small apartment without any air-conditioning. She had to be sweltering.

If she was, she could always go to a movie to cool off. Or a department store.

Or—

At eleven-thirty, he went out to see about buying an air-conditioning unit.

Chapter Six

He kept popping up where she least expected it. First in her life, now on her doorstep.

If she had a doorstep.

But here he was, standing in front of her door, straining under the weight of a huge box, the muscles of his arms budging.

They looked rock hard.

It took her almost a full second to find her tongue. Another second to make use of it. ''Jason, what are you doing here?''

He was bracing the back end of the box against the wall beside her door. Even so, it was still hard to hold it up. Thank God the superintendent had fixed the elevator. He'd forgotten all about that complication until he'd gotten to her building. Carrying this damn thing half a block had been bad enough.

"Right now, working on a hernia." Jason wasn't sure just how much longer he could hold the box up without dropping it. "Open the door farther, Mindy. This thing weighs a ton."

Stunned, Mindy stepped back to let him in, opening the door as far back as she could. She asked, "What is that?" although she could see what was inside by the words slapped all over four sides of the box. What she really meant was what was he doing with it and why was it in her apartment?

Why was *he* in her apartment?

With a huge sigh of relief, Jason placed the box he'd purchased from the major appliance store on the first available place on her floor. For a tiny apartment, it was amazingly uncluttered.

As an afterthought he dropped the navy canvas bag that had been slung over his shoulder. He took a deep breath before answering.

"An air conditioner. Top-of-the line they claim." He'd been dripping since he'd left his car, parked half a block and across the street. "Could I have a glass of water, please?"

"Yes, of course."

What was wrong with her? The man had to be dying. She hurried the five steps over to the sink, eyeing the box all the while. Making sure the water was cold, she filled the glass to the top, then handed it to him.

"But, Jason, I can't—"

"Accept it?" he guessed as he took the glass from her. "Sure you can." Jason paused as he drained the glass. He had no idea lugging the box would take so much out of him. It just reminded him how much he hated the heat. "We need an administrative assistant who's fresh, not wilted when she comes in." He handed the empty glass back to her and took a moment to focus on her face. "As a matter of fact, you look a little green around the gills this morning, and the sun hasn't even hit its peak yet."

He was glad he'd gone with his impulse and hadn't reasoned himself out of the purchase. Whatever had brought her to these circumstances, he wasn't going to allow her pride to prevent her from accepting the unit. She clearly needed it.

He squatted down and began loosening the metal staples that held the box closed.

"In case you haven't noticed, we're in the middle of a heat wave," he told her. "It's ninety-three degrees outside with humidity to match. Hell is cooler. I thought we might even the odds a little."

She circled around the box, tempted even though she knew she shouldn't let him do this. "How did you know I didn't have an air conditioner?"

Working one large copper-colored staple loose, he glanced in her direction. "I'm observant."

He might be observant, but the man didn't have X-ray vision, and her door had only been slightly ajar. "But I didn't let you in the other night."

Yes, you did, a little. He almost said it out loud,

but stopped himself at the last moment. She was talking about the real and not the emotional.

"I looked up when you pointed out where you lived. Since you only have one window and there was nothing hanging from it, I just made the natural leap that you didn't have one of these."

She regarded the large box dubiously. "The super doesn't work on Sundays."

He had a feeling that was the case, so he'd planned on doing the installation himself. "No, but I do."

Even with all those muscles of his, she didn't assume that Jason knew his way around a tool belt. "You're handy?"

"Enough to know which end is up and how to keep it that way."

"My husband—my ex," she amended, "was all thumbs." She laughed shortly. "Not exactly a good thing when you're an octopus." She watched as Jason began to work the second large metal staple out of the cardboard. "Is there anything I can do?"

"Stand out of the way." He opened up the flaps of the box. Beneath it was a wall of packing material. "I don't want to hit you with this."

Mindy shoved her hands into the back pockets of her denim shorts and did as she was told, watching in rapt fascination. Jason's muscles strained as he began to maneuver the unit out of the box. Jumping in, she held down the sides as he pulled out the air conditioner, encased in white Styrofoam.

A bag of nuts and bolts fell out at her feet. She

looked down at them, then bit her lower lip. "I don't have any tools for you to use." That was something she was still meaning to get. At least a couple of screw drivers and a wrench.

Setting the air-conditioning unit on the floor beside the box, Jason nodded at the canvas bag he'd dropped unceremoniously on the floor.

"I've got everything I need in there." He saw the look on her face. It gave him a certain sense of satisfaction to be one up on her ex-husband. "I learned that in the Boy Scouts. Always Be Prepared."

Squatting, she opened the bag and saw that he had all manner of tools inside.

Manly, she thought. But then she already knew that. However, he had given her a piece of information she hadn't known before. "You were a Boy Scout?"

"For six months." Jason worked the foam away from the sides of the unit. Beneath it, the air conditioner was wrapped in plastic. He sighed, angling the unit and removing the sheeting. "My mother thought it might help me fit in."

Some people, she thought, weren't meant to fit in. They were meant to stand out. "What happened after six months?"

Jason lifted one shoulder in a vague shrug. "I didn't fit in. She gave up."

Mindy thought of his firm and the reputation it had. Living well, she'd once heard, was the best revenge. "You fit in now."

He still thought of himself as that kid who marched out of tune. "If you say so."

She sat back on her heels, looking at him. Was he serious? He was. It amazed her that someone who looked like Jason, who had come as far as he had, didn't have a vain bone in his body. "All sorts of people come to you, asking for your advice. I've only been there a week and I'm really impressed with what you can do."

He stopped sorting the various nuts and screws to look at her. "That goes both ways." In response, he saw color creep up her cheeks. "Looks like I brought this thing just in time."

Mindy moved back a little, although there wasn't enough space to make a difference. "What do you mean?"

"Your cheeks are getting pink." He put the instruction sheets in proper order. "First green, then pink." Jason grinned at her, then emptied the canvas bag, setting the tools down on the rug. "You're a veritable rainbow."

She felt a little self-conscious. "And you're a positive chatterbox compared to the rest of the week. Do you become another person on Sundays?"

He shrugged. Rising, he picked up the air conditioner and brought it over to her open window. With a little work, the fit would be perfect. "Maybe you bring out the vocabulary in me." He braced the unit with his hip. "Hand me that wrench, will you?"

Jason was holding his hand out, his attention focused on the air conditioner, which was precariously perched in the window. He braced it in place with his other hand.

Grabbing the wrench from the small array of tools on the floor, Mindy scrambled to her feet. She placed the tool in his hand, her fingertips making contact with his palm. He turned his head and looked at her for a long moment. "Thanks."

She smiled, a warm feeling coming in from all sides and hugging her. "You're welcome."

Inspired by her presence and the fact that it was incredibly hot, Jason worked quickly. Even though he'd never installed one before, it took him a relatively short time to get the air-conditioning unit up and running. He'd discovered he had a natural aptitude when it came to things like this.

The change inside Mindy's apartment was immediate. The small studio went from being a sauna to deliciously comfortable in less than five minutes.

Jason felt pretty satisfied with himself as he looked at her. "There, how's that?"

Mindy stood in front of the unit, letting the cold air swirl around her. Her eyes all but fluttered shut in pure ecstasy.

"Wonderful." She turned to look at him, a smile playing on her lips. "You realize, of course, I may never come into work now. I won't want to leave the apartment to hit the streets."

He began putting the tools back into the worn bag.

''Once you get the first electricity bill, you will. That is, if you want to keep paying for the luxury of not being fricasseed.''

She joined him on the floor, helping him gather up his tools. It only took a couple of minutes before they were done. She rocked back on her heels. ''I'll pay you back, you know, first check.''

Jason nodded. He supposed it was better that way. Kept the lines drawn between them.

''I never doubted it. No hurry, though. I know where you live.'' On his feet, he offered her his hand. As she rose, she brushed up against him.

All sorts of signals went flashing through him. He felt his body tightening like a bow about to fire off an arrow.

He cleared his throat. ''Not much room in here.''

He felt it, too, she thought. That wild electrical impulse that seemed to travel between them. ''I think the real estate woman called it cozy.''

He nodded, picking up the bag. Telling himself he had to go. Standing rooted to the spot. ''That's what they usually say when there's not enough room to turn around in a place.''

''Oh, there's enough room. See?''

She purposely turned around to prove her point. But the quick action, despite the cooled state of the apartment, made her feel slightly dizzy and light-headed. Coming to the end of the turn, she wavered just a little. Just enough to make Jason reach out to catch her, afraid she might fall.

"Yeah, I see. No more impromptu dancing, understand? Unless it's slow dancing." Every word left his lips in slow motion.

The tempo was in direct contrast to his heart, which had gone into double time the moment he'd caught her. The moment he had her against him.

He wanted to kiss her again.

But he couldn't. He didn't want her to think that he'd come here with an ulterior motive. That he meant to trade his labor for something, using the air conditioner as some kind of bargaining chip.

He'd honestly come here with good intentions, he wanted her to know that. The best way was to leave. Now.

That meant he had to let her go.

Easier said than done.

"I'll keep that in mind," she told him softly.

Her body felt as if someone had just lit a match to it. It took everything she had not to put her head against his chest. She knew she would have found that infinitely comforting.

Not exactly something a woman who's trying to be independent would do, she upbraided herself.

Mindy looked up at him. "Can I make you brunch?" she whispered.

What he wanted her to do was make him happy, for perhaps the first time in his life. But that was moving in a direction he couldn't afford to go in.

With reluctance Jason released her. "No, I've got some things to do."

Disappointed, she forced a smile to her lips. "Other air conditioners to install?"

"No." Barely avoiding tripping over the canvas bag, he picked it up. He'd almost forgotten it. "Yours was the only one for today. I'd better go." Before I can't, he added silently. "I'll see you tomorrow."

She followed him to the door. "Fresh, not wilted," she agreed. "Jason—"

His hand already on the doorknob, he turned to look at her. "Yes?"

"Thank you."

Impulsively, because he'd been thoughtful in ways her husband never had been, she rose up on her toes and brushed a quick kiss along Jason's cheek. And then didn't back away.

Going with impulses himself, with needs that seemed to be barely under wraps when it came to her, Jason took her into his arms and kissed her the way he wanted to.

The way she wanted him to.

Jason kissed her for a long, long moment, one filled with all sorts of unuttered promises. And then, because he knew that if he continued kissing her for another half beat of his heart he wasn't going to let it end there, he stopped.

"I'd better—"

"Yeah," she breathed, knowing what he was saying. What he was thinking. Because it was what she was thinking, too.

While she wanted it, while she hoped that he

wanted it, too, she knew that giving in to what she was feeling would only vastly complicate her life, which was already too complicated.

So, with a feeling of deep regret, she moved back, away from him, on legs that felt oddly wooden, given the nature of the rest of her body. Which was still on fire. And then she closed the door to keep herself from going after him again.

Because she knew she would, given half a chance.

With a sigh she went over to her sofa and sank down. Despite the temperature the air conditioner was set on, it took her a long time to cool down.

"So, tell me, has she managed to finally win you over yet?"

Deeply immersed in working on his monthly newsletter, it took a moment for the husky-voiced question to penetrate the wall around him. When it did, Jason looked up to see Nathalie walking into his office.

There was a glow about her, the kind she sported whenever she was falling in love. It looked as if things were going well between her and her latest conquest, he thought. When Nathalie was in love, she wanted the whole world to be the same. That inevitably included him. Usually he found that to be annoying. But right now he realized he wasn't as resistant to the idea as he usually was.

He should be, but he wasn't.

He tried to play her words over, but couldn't. "Did you just say something?"

Nathalie crossed to his desk, a knowing smile on her lips. He shifted restlessly in his chair, the ergonomic one she'd selected for him. Nathalie had an uncanny knack of being able to read people. He could read stock trends, absorbing all the nuances and finally making sense out of them while she could do the same with people. That was what made them such a good team.

Right now he had a feeling that she knew everything about his weekend, incredibly tame though it was in comparison to anything she might have done.

"The new girl. Mindy." Nathalie deliberately said her name slowly. "Has she won you over yet?" Cocking her head, she studied him for a second. Then, before he could reply, she hurried on, "Isn't she everything we ever hoped for?"

He looked at the small pile beside his stock trend data. Mindy's pile. There were reports on almost everything that had to do with the office and the business. In a matter of a week, Mindy had broken down the staff's activities, given him an accurate assessment of where everyone was on their projects, had done the payroll, had arranged both his and Nathalie's schedules for the coming week and, in short, done everything Nathalie had promised and made herself indispensable.

As if Mindy had to lift a finger to accomplish the latter.

Still, if he told Nathalie that she'd been right all

along immediately, he would never hear the end of it. ''You could say that.''

Nathalie laughed, patting him on the shoulder as if he was a star pupil.

''I do say that. The trick is to get *you* to say that.'' She leaned over and looked him in the eye. Bearding the lion in his den, she called it. ''Say it, Jason. Say that Mindy Richards is everything we could have hoped for in an administrative assistant.''

Jason leaned back in his chair and scrutinized his partner. She looked higher on happiness than he'd ever seen her. And he had seen Nathalie through two marriages and numerous affairs. ''What the hell did you do this weekend?''

Her smile, hardly inscrutable but somehow still mysterious for all that, seemed to spread all over her face, taking in every feature. Her laugh was deep and incredibly suggestive.

''A more easy question to answer is what *didn't* we do this weekend.''

Jason pretended to cover his ears. ''Too much information, Nathalie, you're giving me too much information. I really don't need to hear this.''

''Oh, but you do.'' Playing along, Nathalie pulled his hands away from his head. ''It might inspire you to leave the comfort of your dry statistical world and live life in, if not the fast lane, at least the lane that isn't queuing up to get off the freeway at the very first exit it comes to.''

To punctuate her statement, she turned the monitor screen away from him.

Slanting a warning look in her direction, Jason turned the monitor back. "Nathalie, in case you haven't noticed, those dry statistics and my reading them is what keeps clients coming back to us for advice."

It was obvious that this morning she wasn't in the mood to listen to reason. "Yes, yes, I know. But all work and no play—"

He knew where she was driving, and even though he wanted to make the trip there himself, he resisted. He believed in hard work, not risks, and putting himself out there, exposed, definitely fell into the risk category.

"—make Mallory and Dixon a profitable company."

Nathalie was nothing if not tenacious. They'd gotten their best clients that way. This time, it was his chair she moved instead of his monitor. She angled it to face her.

"Nowhere in the company charter does it state that you have to remain a monk forever."

Surrendering, for the moment, the physical aspect of the battle, he pinned Nathalie with a look. "Just exactly how did this go from a conversation about my admitting that the new girl you hired is turning out all right, to my love life?"

Nathalie sighed dramatically, then allowed a mischievous smile to play on her lips.

"You don't *have* a love life, Jason, that's precisely my point. I want you to have one." Her eyes were sparkling with memories of the weekend. "I want you to be happy."

This time he regained possession of his chair and turned it back to his desk. "If you want me to be happy, go back to your office and talk to our clients while I go over this and give you something to talk about. The newsletter has to go out."

She sighed again, withdrawing. For now. She paused in the doorway to give him a final warning. "I'm not giving up, you know."

"I know," he sighed.

The problem was, Jason mused, looking down at the yet-unfinished newsletter, she had more of a chance of getting him as a convert than she thought.

With renewed determination, Jason turned his mind to his work. And only allowed the feel of soft lips against his to break into his thoughts every ten minutes instead of every five.

Chapter Seven

He was at a loss as to how to end it.

Jason leaned back in his chair, rocking slightly as he looked at the flat-panel screen on his desk. More specifically, at the monthly newsletter he'd been laboring over off and on for the past two days.

Despite the summaries he'd gotten from his interns and his own almost constant monitoring of stock market trends and endless reading of all the latest investment articles, writing this month's letter was a bear.

No pun intended, he amended mentally.

It was certainly giving him a harder time than usual to put together.

He glanced toward his closed door and was at a

loss. Lately the only pattern he'd been able to come up with for the various stocks, bonds, mutual funds and securities that were part of the market was that there *was* no pattern. Or at least, not one that was clear by any means.

With a sigh, he pulled closer to the keyboard and typed the short, terse paragraph in which he gave his conclusion.

There, done.

The usual sense of satisfaction that came whenever he put one of these newsletters to bed didn't arrive this time. Jason frowned.

He hoped that he was giving his clients their money's worth. It wasn't in him just to take the money and run. He always gave his work his all. That included the personal advice he gave to various clients as well as his monthly newsletter that had a healthy circulation of over 75,000 subscribers. They relied on him, and he wanted to deliver.

Trouble was, in this day and age of global unrest and uncertainty, it was hard to predict just what the market was going to do.

Ordinarily, he could weather the storms. He'd found that he'd always had a gift for this sort of thing, a natural interest in seeing how various companies did on the market, a knack for being able to predict with more than a fair amount of accuracy just what was going to happen. Trading had fascinated him ever since he could remember.

He supposed that had always set him apart from most people. He wasn't interested in parties or loud music or meaningless exchanges about easily forgotten subjects with people he'd probably never see again. He never had been.

Maybe that was why Debra had lost interest in him so soon after the wedding.

He scrolled to the beginning of his newsletter and ran a spell check on it.

Debra probably would have lost interest in him before the wedding if she hadn't pressed so hard for a quick union, he thought. She'd wanted to get married right from the start. She was beautiful and persuasive, and he'd completely lost his head and his perspective. She'd told him that she saw things in him. It made him feel ten feet tall to have the debutante/campus beauty queen pay exclusive attention to him.

And three inches tall to discover that she had lovers, even as she shrank from his touch.

He should have realized that the match was doomed from the start. Two different worlds hardly ever merged. And that, he supposed, was his problem. He tended to be drawn to the unattainable.

Mindy had been like that in high school. Unattainable. From the best home, a child of privilege. Someone who could look at him and not even see him at all because he wasn't on the A list.

Except that now he was, he thought, even though he didn't feel it. And from what she'd told him, Mindy no longer was on that list.

Odd how their roles had gotten reversed. His feelings about her certainly hadn't. If anything they had become more intense.

But he was still behaving like that kid in high school, he thought. That kid who hadn't enough nerve to ask the golden girl out.

Time, he decided, to put that behind him.

They'd shared a cup of coffee and an air conditioner installation. Combined, that almost qualified as a date, didn't it?

There was nothing preventing him from taking the next step, he told himself. Asking her out for a real date. To a restaurant or, better yet, to the theater. He had a feeling that Mindy liked seeing plays.

He made a mental note to get two tickets to the biggest hit on Broadway. The producer was a client of his. Scoring two front-row-center seats shouldn't be much of a problem.

This was the way to go; he was sure of it. He smiled. There was an active attraction there, on her part as well as on his. He'd felt it. He just had to open his mouth and say the words.

Mindy, are you busy Friday night?

Nothing hard about that, was there?

Then why the hell did his pulse rate just go up a notch, even though he was still sitting by himself in his office?

Exasperated with himself, Jason pressed the key combination that would save his work to disk, then popped it out of the computer. Leaving it on his desk, he pressed down the intercom button on his multilined phone. He heard it buzz in the outer office.

Here goes everything. "Mindy, can I see you in my office, please?"

He waited for her affirmation. Instead, he heard a soft knock on his door.

Every nerve in his body tightened.

He'd felt less apprehensive at the last seminar he'd addressed, and there had been almost a thousand people in the auditorium.

"Come in."

Mindy walked into the room. Her clothes, a short-sleeved white blouse and navy-blue straight short skirt, looked crisper than she did. Despite her smile, she looked a little wan.

Was she still working too hard, trying to prove herself to him? It wasn't necessary. He'd put her through a number of hoops last week, but this week had been relatively light. Having made the decision that he really wanted her to stay, he'd gone out of his way to make sure she wasn't overwhelmed.

She looked positively pale as she asked, "What can I do for you?"

So many things you can't even begin to guess. The answer popped into his head without so much as a preamble. He was grateful she didn't claim to possess the gift of mind reading.

If Nathalie had been in the room, he wouldn't have felt as relieved. There were times, he could swear, his partner was part witch. Or at least marginally clairvoyant.

He held up the gray disk. "I need this to go to Adam, the desktop publisher," he added, in case she didn't know who he was referring to.

She did, and he had referred to the man by the wrong name. ''Allen,'' she corrected.

''Right, Allen.'' He knew that. Didn't he? Who was he kidding? He knew every single stock that was currently available, along with its abbreviation, by heart, but when it came to keeping the names of his employees straight, he only had a fifty-fifty chance of being right. ''Tell Allen it's the newsletter. He's been waiting for it. Remind him it needs to reach the distribution department by tomorrow morning.''

She took the disk from him and was already on her way out. ''You got it.''

Okay, now, ask her out now. He sucked in his courage, knowing that he'd rather face a tribe of disgruntled investors than go through this.

''And Mindy?''

At the door she turned around again. The room turned with her.

Mindy tried to grab the doorknob to steady herself. And missed. All morning, she'd had this strange, twilight-type feeling. She would have said it was the heat, but between the air-conditioning in her apartment, the office and the bus she'd ridden to work, she'd hardly had time to feel it. This was something else. Something that seemed to have latched on to her and insisted on making the edges of her world fuzzy.

Except, now the edges of her world were getting smaller and smaller, being eaten up by an inkiness she couldn't push back, couldn't hold at bay.

It was threatening to swallow her up.

''Mindy, are you all right?''

Somewhere in the far recesses of her world, she could hear Jason's voice. He was asking her something, but she couldn't make out the words. They buzzed around her head like tiny bees.

She could feel perspiration popping up all over her brow.

Her knees were leaving her.

The room was leaving her.

And then there was nothing.

Horrified, Jason watched Mindy's eyes roll back in her head and saw her begin to crumple. Leaping from his chair and around his desk, he managed to reach her just before she hit the floor.

He held her against him like a rag doll. She was completely limp.

And he was completely lost.

"Nathalie!" he yelled, then raised his voice even higher and called out his partner's name again.

Nathalie hurried into his office a minute later. "You bellowed?" Her mouth dropped open when she saw him holding the unconscious woman in his arms. "My God, Jason, what are you doing?"

"Keeping her from hitting the floor. She fainted," he added helplessly.

The initial shock passed quickly, fading into the background. Sweeping into his office, Nathalie went to the sofa and moved aside the vivid blue afghan she'd given him as a joke last Christmas.

"Relax. Put her down here. This kind of thing happens all the time."

He threw Nathalie a look as he gently placed

Mindy on the couch. She was still boneless, and he was getting really worried. "Not around me."

"It has nothing to do with you," Nathalie told him. Just as a precaution she placed her hand to Mindy's forehead. It was cool. Which brought her back to her original suspicion. "I'll go get a wet towel."

But he wanted to hear more of an explanation. Jason caught his partner by the wrist. "What do you mean it happens all the time?"

She didn't bother to disengage herself. Jason was overreacting, but then, he was a male. It took the species time to come to their senses. "Some pregnant women faint in their early trimesters."

"Pregnant?" He stared at Mindy, utterly stunned. Nathalie had to be wrong. Mindy couldn't be pregnant. "What makes you think she's pregnant?" Belatedly he let go of Nathalie's wrist.

"Well, for one thing, I've got a gift for being able to intuit things about people—" then she smiled "—and for another, she told me."

Everything inside of him went completely numb. "She's pregnant," he repeated.

There was something in his manner that got to the single maternal chord within Nathalie's makeup. Her voice softened as she looked at him. "Yes, honey, she's pregnant. Didn't she tell you?"

His expression was stony as he stared at the unconscious woman on his sofa. "It never came up."

Guilt needled at her. "Sorry, maybe I should have mentioned it."

He looked at her, his eyes blazing. "Damn it, yes, you should have mentioned it."

Nathalie did a complete retraction. "Maybe I shouldn't have said anything now, seeing the way you're reacting."

Pregnant. Mindy was pregnant. There was another man's child growing within her. Jason felt as if all the pieces on the chessboard he'd arranged so carefully had just been upended.

"Are you sure?"

Of course Nathalie was sure, he upbraided himself. Why would Mindy lie to her about something like that? Desperate, he grasped on to the memory that she'd said something about women wearing wedding rings to keep people from hitting on them....

Still, there was no reason for her to have told Nathalie she was pregnant. If she wasn't.

Nathalie laid a hand on his shoulder. He let it stay. "Afraid so."

It hurt him to breathe. To think. "How—how far along is she?"

"Three months, she said," Nathalie told him softly. "I know, she doesn't show at all." Cocking her head, she looked at Mindy's slender form. "And by now she should, seeing as how she's carrying twins."

He looked at her sharply. "Twins?" This was just getting better and better.

"Twins," she repeated. "As in two babies."

Bitterness emerged out of nowhere and welled up inside of him. He stared at Mindy, addressing his words to Nathalie, who should have warned him. "Anything else you want to tell me?"

"Not that I can think of." Several people had gathered at the doorway, looking in. "Nothing to see, people." She shooed the interns away. "Go back to your desks. She's going to be fine. Just a little heat stroke."

He wished Nathalie had said that to him. But then, this wasn't the kind of thing that could have been hidden indefinitely. It was better to know the truth. He'd almost done something very stupid.

"Feel free to drop another bomb on me at any time," he muttered in Nathalie's direction as she hurried out of the room to get the wet towel.

Feeling oddly hollow, Jason sat down on the edge of the sofa beside Mindy. He checked her pulse. It was racing. That couldn't be good. Maybe he should get her to a doctor for an examination.

And maybe while he was at it, he should get his own head examined.

What the hell had he been thinking?

Nathalie was back in less time than it had taken him to rake himself over the coals. She must have run, to get to the bathroom and back this fast.

"Here." She handed him a wet towel. "Put this on her forehead."

He took it from her and folded it before placing it on Mindy's forehead. "I know where it goes, Nathalie, I'm not that stupid."

"No one said you were stupid, Jason. Just a little dense sometimes," Nathalie added fondly.

The instant the cool, wet towel touched her forehead, Mindy's eyes fluttered open. They were wide with surprise as she looked up at Jason.

Struggling, she tried to sit up. "What—what happened?"

Very gently Jason pushed her back down. "Don't try to get up just yet. You fainted." And he was afraid of a repeat performance.

She remembered nothing beyond standing at the doorway and feeling the room sway. "I what?"

"You fainted," he repeated. "I caught you before you could hit your head on the floor." He felt betrayed, concerned and a host of other feelings he couldn't even sort out. They were all going around in a dizzying circle. But first and foremost, he wanted to be sure Mindy was all right. "Do you want to see your doctor?"

She moved her head slightly from side to side. The dizziness, mercifully, was retreating. "No."

Well, he couldn't very well force her to go, although he would have felt better if she went. But there was something he did have control over. "All right, then I'll take you home."

"No." This time her voice had more conviction in it as she protested.

With the wisdom of someone who knew when they were a witness to something they shouldn't be, Nathalie began to ease out of the room.

"I'll just leave you two to sort this out by yourselves." She looked at Jason. "I'll be in my office if you need me. Just bellow like the last time." Her brown eyes shifted to Mindy. "That goes for you, too.

And don't let him intimidate you. His bark is worse than his bite.''

Jason looked at the disk that was still clutched in Mindy's fingers. ''Here, do something positive.'' He still hadn't forgiven her for not telling him about Mindy in the first place. ''Take this to Allen for me.''

Nathalie looked at him, wondering if it was just a coincidence. ''Hey, you remembered his name. There's hope for you yet.''

He wasn't about to take credit when none was due, even for something as minor as this. ''Mindy corrected me.''

''Knew there had to be a reason.'' Nathalie laughed and shook her head. She held up the disk. ''I'll see this gets to him right away.''

Stepping out of the office, she closed the door behind her, giving them privacy.

He wanted to yell at Mindy, to shake her by her shoulders. But he knew that was unreasonable. It was only his wounded pride making him overreact. ''Why didn't you tell me?''

Mindy ventured into a semisitting position, propping herself up on her elbows. ''Tell you what?''

''That you were pregnant.''

She looked at him apprehensively. Was he going to fire her? His was the first name on the door and he had as much weight as Nathalie when it came to hiring and firing. Probably more. ''I told Nathalie.''

''That's not the same thing.'' He struggled to hold on to his temper, but it wasn't easy. Damn it, she should have said something. "I wouldn't have kissed you if I knew that you were pregnant."

"Why? It's not catching." She blew out a breath, utterly flustered, then chewed on her bottom lip. She'd known she would have to let Jason know about her condition eventually, but this wasn't the way she'd wanted him to find out. Gathering her thoughts together, she decided to tell him the truth. "I didn't tell you because I was embarrassed."

He frowned, underscoring his confusion. "Embarrassed?"

She sat up, swinging her legs off the sofa. Still a little unsteady, she decided to sit a few minutes longer. "I didn't want to look like a fool." Not knowing what he could be thinking, she slanted a glance at him. "You know, pregnant, dumped, that kind of thing."

She still wasn't making any sense. "As I recall, you told me you dumped him. And he deserved it."

He'd get no argument from her on that score. Still, it did leave her in a predicament. "The end result is still the same. Pregnant and alone."

She would never be alone as long as he was around. Even if things couldn't turn out the way he would have liked them to. "Nathalie said you were carrying twins."

She looked down at her still-flat stomach. "That's what the doctor said."

"And he knew this?" It seemed incredible to him. How could a man walk away from his family, from his responsibilities? ''Your husband knew this and he still—''

Not that Brad deserved any consideration, but since she was telling Jason the truth, she didn't want him getting any of the details wrong.

''Brad knows I'm pregnant, but he doesn't know it's twins. I just found that out when I moved back to Manhattan.'' Her mother's gynecologist had confirmed the findings. Just by coincidence she'd run into the sister of an old friend who happened to be working at Manhattan Multiples. She'd decided to give them a try. So far it was the best decision she'd made, other than leaving Brad. ''It seems one baby was hiding behind the other on the first sonogram that was taken. Not hard when they're the size of sunflower seeds.'' She sighed and looked at him. ''I'm sorry I fainted.''

''Not exactly something you had any control over.'' He wanted to hold her, to put his arm around her shoulders and just comfort her. But he did neither. ''Are you sure you don't want to go to see a doctor?''

She smiled, liking the sound of concern in his voice. Brad could stand to learn a great deal from Jason. ''I'm sure.''

''But I am taking you home.''

There was no nonsense in his voice, but she wasn't going to be railroaded by a man any longer, even if that man was Jason.

''No, really, I'm fine.'' She saw that he was unconvinced. ''Please, Jason, I need to be busy. I need to be doing something.''

He frowned slightly, still feeling as if he'd been betrayed. ''Seems to me producing several hundred cells a day—times two—should be enough.''

She held up her hand, as if to ward off what he was saying. ''No metaphysical philosophy, Jason. If all I wanted to do was sit around and be pregnant, I could have taken my parents up on their offer to dote on me. But I didn't,'' she emphasized. ''Lots of women out there are doing exactly what I'm doing. Single women. Having babies, raising them alone.'' She looked at Jason, her eyes entreating him to understand. ''Don't think I'm not grateful, Jason, but don't treat me like a child. I'm a woman.''

That was just the problem, he thought. He was incredibly aware that she was. And it kept getting in the way of everything.

Chapter Eight

Mindy was concentrating so hard on the calculations she was doing, she didn't see the young blonde until the latter was almost on top of her.

''Hello, I'm Gloria Honeycutt.'' The woman's Southern drawl was thick and soothing. Her blue eyes swept over her desk, as if she was trying to make an assessment. ''Where would you like me to start?''

Mindy stared at her, utterly confused. She recognized the woman as one of the interns who worked on summarizing various data coming in from the reliable sources Jason used to form his predictions. But that didn't explain what she was doing here, or her question. ''Excuse me?''

''To start. To help.'' When that didn't seem to

strike a chord, it was Gloria's turn to look puzzled. "Didn't they tell you?"

"Tell me what?"

But even as Mindy asked, she braced herself for the inevitable words she felt had to be coming. She was fired. Terminated. Released with thanks, but waved on her way because her belly was soon going to rival that of Santa Claus after an eating binge.

This was only the first step. First help, then take over. Then the door. But she'd been so sure she was doing well. Just yesterday Jason had actually complimented her on a job well done.

Gloria nodded over her head toward the door leading into Jason's office. "Mr. Mallory sent me over to see if I could take some of the load off your shoulders. Said you might not be feeling well."

So that was it. She wasn't being fired. Relief flooded through her. "No load," Mindy assured her. "Shoulders are fine." She raised and lowered them to underline the point. "And I'm fine."

The confusion in the other woman's eyes increased. She looked at her doubtfully. It was obvious that what she was hearing wasn't jibing with what she'd been told. "Are you sure? Mr. Mallory seemed to think that you had too much to do."

Mindy wasn't sure whether to be touched or insulted. In either case, none of this was the blonde's fault. "I'm like Goldilocks after the third try. I have exactly enough to do. But, thanks. I'll call you if it gets to be too much."

Gloria hesitated, her expression uncertain. And then she nodded. ‘‘Okay.’’ She leaned over Mindy’s desk and tapped the list of extensions taped to the face of the multilined phone with a bright blue nail. ‘‘My extension’s right there. Gloria Honeycutt,’’ she repeated.

‘‘Got it.’’

Mindy waited until the blonde disappeared around the corner, then gathered her indignation to her. It made the perfect shield.

As a rule Mindy wasn’t the confrontational type, but maybe it was time she learned. There wasn’t going to be anyone to fight her battles for her. Moreover, in less than six months she was going to have to fight battles for her babies, as well. There was no use in putting off her first foray. Besides, she had a number of things to drop off with Jason, anyway. She pulled them into a pile and picked them up.

Getting up from her desk, she squared her shoulders and went to beard the lion in his expensive den.

Her arms filled with files and reports, Mindy still managed to knock and open Jason’s door at the same time. ‘‘Gloria Honeycutt just came to my desk. She said you sent her.’’

Jason looked up from his work. She got his full attention immediately. There was an expression on Mindy’s face he couldn’t quite read. Was she annoyed or just stressed?

‘‘I did,’’ he replied slowly.

He saw her eyes narrow over the bridge of her perfect little nose as she regarded him. "Why?"

"You're pregnant."

"Yes?" Impatience slipped into her tone, even though she'd meant to hold it under wraps.

"So I thought you might want some help."

She deliberately put on an innocent expression. "In being pregnant? If you can get someone to take over my morning sickness, I'd appreciate it. And a surrogate backache person would be great. But my fingers are all in working order and so's my mind—the pregnancy hasn't gotten to them yet." She leaned forward over his desk, determined to make her point. "So unless you have some kind of complaint about my work—" She looked at him, silently praying he wasn't going to find fault with anything.

"I don't."

With a sense of relief, she straightened and tossed her head, her long black, shining hair flying over her shoulder. "Then let me do my job, please."

She was offended, he realized. Didn't she understand that he was only trying to help her? "Mindy, this is a difficult time for you—"

How would he know? How would he even have a clue what this time was like for her? He'd never been left feeling unattractive, unloved.

"Then don't make it any more difficult by making me doubt my abilities." She sighed. "I thought we already had this talk on Tuesday, after you found out about my condition."

"I thought you were just paying lip service, saying what you thought I wanted to hear."

Typical man, putting his own weird spin on what he thought was being said to him. She supposed she couldn't fault him, really. As far as men went, he was a hell of a lot better model than her husband had been. Her ex, her ex, she reminded herself. She was going to have to remember that. The papers had come in the mail and she'd signed them, sending them on their way. It was official. She was a single woman again. A single, pregnant woman.

"I'll let you know when I'm saying something I think you just want to hear." That settled, she turned her attention to the things she'd brought in with her. "Now, here's your schedule for next week." She placed it in front of him. It had taken her time to make sense out of the notes on his calendar. She knew that if he didn't have this in front of him, according to Nathalie, he was liable to make two appointments for the same time. "The payroll's done for Friday and the checks just need your signature." She placed this batch beside the schedule. "Oh, and don't forget, you have a conference call with David Manning, the CEO at WorldSpeak, at three." She lifted her chin triumphantly as she looked at him. "There, is that efficient enough for you?"

"Yes." He grinned as he pulled the checks closer. "Very."

"Good. Now if you'll excuse me," she began to

withdraw from the room, "I think I have to throw up."

Jason was on his feet in an instant. "I can—"

She laughed and shook her head. Who would ever have thought that the brooding high school bad boy would be such a pushover when it came to this kind of thing? In a way, she supposed, it renewed her faith in men. Or at least in this particular man.

Mindy waved him back to his chair. "Just kidding, Jason. My morning sickness disappears promptly at seven every morning, thank God." She opened the door to leave. "Now, if you need anything else, you know where to find me." Mindy stepped over the threshold. "At my desk—working."

With that, she closed the door, feeling immensely satisfied with herself.

Just before three o'clock, Nathalie walked into his office holding a cut-glass vase that sported a red ribbon around it. An effusion of long-stemmed, red roses was tucked inside. She didn't bother knocking, but then, she never did.

She held the vase aloft for him to see. "I just got these."

He raised his eyes from the notes he was making to himself. He had a few minutes left before his call went through and he wanted to be prepared. "Very nice."

Nathalie twirled the end of the bright red ribbon

around her index finger. ‘‘And they’re not from Paolo.’’

He didn’t do innocence well, but he gave it a stab. ‘‘No?’’

She put the vase down on his desk. ‘‘Why did you send me roses, Jason?’’

He put his pen down and rocked back in his chair. The florist had done a nice job with his selection, he thought. ‘‘You like them and I wanted to say thank you.’’

Nathalie cocked her head. ‘‘For?’’

He was certain she knew the answer to that, but he humored her. ‘‘Hiring Mindy.’’

She grinned, her eyes disappearing into darkly lashed crescents. ‘‘So, you’re finally going to admit I did a good thing?’’

He never lavished praise, but he believed in giving credit where it was due. ‘‘You always do good things, Nathalie. This just happens to be a little better than usual.’’

‘‘She’s a live one, isn’t she?’’

Mindy had always been ‘‘a live one.’’ It was the way she’d developed that impressed him. ‘‘Hard to believe it’s the same girl I knew in high school.’’

‘‘I thought you two didn’t mix it up.’’ Crossing her arms in front of her, Nathalie leaned her hip against the desk, waiting for details.

‘‘We didn’t.’’ He tried to summarize it for her. ‘‘But she was the head cheerleader—’’

Nathalie raised a hand to stop him. ‘‘Say no more,

I know what that means. Perfect everything.'' Closing her eyes, she shuddered. ''She was the kind of girl I want to run over with my dad's Mac truck when I was in high school. Cheerleader, huh?'' Life was funny at times. Good thing there was no room for that on their application form, she thought. ''If I'd known that, I might not have hired her.'' She looked pointedly at him. ''And then we all would have lost.''

He knew he shouldn't have given in to his impulse and sent the roses. ''Go back to your office and take your roses with you, Nathalie. I've got a conference call coming in.''

''Already gone.'' But she wasn't. She was standing several feel shy of the door, chewing on a thought. ''Jason…''

He knew that tone. One hand on his notes, Jason raised his eyes warily to his partner. ''What?''

Nathalie's eyes were bright with possibilities. ''Why don't you take her with you?''

Exactly what was she driving at? ''To any place in particular?''

She looked at him as if he had suddenly become simpleminded on her. ''To the convention at the Hyatt this weekend.''

All the phrases about borrowing trouble jumped into his head. ''No.''

Hot on the idea, Nathalie wasn't about to give up. ''I can't make it and she'd be perfect.''

''No.'' The very tone was meant to cut her off at the knees. He should have known better.

Nathalie set the vase back down on his desk, one hand on his shoulder as if she could press the notion into his head.

"Jason, stop and think for a second. She's young, she's charming, she draws people in like flies and you could use a little charm on your arm. God knows you were shortchanged in that department."

She was only restating the obvious. His people skills had improved considerably, but he was the first to admit that charming was not a word anyone would ever use to describe him. "Thanks a lot."

If his tone dripped of iciness, Nathalie didn't indicate that she was aware of it.

"Face it, people come to you for your expertise, not your outgoing personality. A little one-two punch doesn't hurt." Nathalie pressed on like a person with right on their side. "Get the CEOs to open up to you. We could always use more input and more clients."

She didn't have to tell him that. It was his own personal mantra. However, he was smart enough to know when he was being asked to play with matches beside a bone-dry forest.

Jason shook his head. "Not a good idea, Nathalie."

She seemed determined to talk him into it. "It's a fabulous idea. I'm not asking you to marry the woman, just take her with you to the conference. Book separate rooms in separate hotels on opposite sides of the convention center if you don't trust yourself."

If looks could kill, Nathalie would have become at

least seriously ill from the glare he sent her. ''It's not a matter of not trusting myself.''

Her eyes held his. Hers had a knowing light in them. ''Isn't it?''

The phone rang, mercifully cutting any further conversation short. ''That's my call.'' He reached for the receiver. Nathalie gave no indication of leaving. ''I'll think about it.''

Hearing that, she picked up her vase and walked out. ''That's all I ask.''

No, he thought as she shut the door behind her, Nathalie might not know it, but she was asking for a lot more.

He thought about leaving them on his desk until the morning. But that would place an undue rush on the process. An undue rush on Mindy.

He thought about doing them himself, but after their last verbal go-round, he didn't want Mindy thinking that he didn't trust her to process the contracts herself. He'd already promised her that he wouldn't call in the temps, or the marines, or anyone else to help her with her job unless she asked him to. That included having him jump into the fray.

What it boiled down to was that he needed to drop off the contracts at her place tonight.

Which was why he found himself circling her block at almost seven o'clock, trying to find a place to safely park both his car and his mind. The car was by far the easy part.

Mindy answered her doorbell on the first ring, but then, there weren't that many square feet for her to cross from any direction except perhaps the fire escape.

"Yes?"

Why did the sound of her disembodied voice do that to him, make his stomach tighten as if he was a prize fighter, anticipating taking a hard punch to the gut? You'd think at his age, with one marriage behind him, he would have been over that.

"It's Jason. I've got more work for you."

He heard her laugh. The sound filled the small foyer and went right through him. His gut tightened another two notches.

"Come on up." She buzzed him in.

The air-conditioning in the hall, he noticed, was working. So was the elevator. It was there, on the first floor, waiting for him. The gods, apparently, were smiling on her building.

He reached her floor before he could rehearse what he was going to say to her. Mindy was standing in her doorway, waiting for him. Looking better than any daydream had a right to look.

Jason blew out a breath as he tried to organize his thoughts. They were scattering like so many laboratory mice when their cages were accidentally thrown open.

"Hi." Mindy stepped back from the door, holding it open for him.

She was wearing cutoff jeans and a light-blue

T-shirt. Try as he might, he couldn't discern any extra weight on her at all. Where was she keeping those babies she was supposed to be carrying? In a bureau drawer?

"Hi," he echoed as he crossed the threshold. "I brought you the Melbourne contracts. I'm going to need them by tomorrow. Morning if possible." He turned to look at her. "Unless you're going out tonight—"

It occurred to him that he had absolutely no idea what her social life was like. Only what he wanted it to be like.

Closing the door, she flipped the lock and then turned to face him.

"Not unless there's a fire drill in the building." She cut the distance between them in four steps and held out her hand for the envelope that was tucked under his arm. When he surrendered it to her, she ran her fingers along the surface. "Still warm."

Something far warmer than the envelope sprang up in his chest. "Not in here, though." When all else fails, talk about the weather, he thought. "Feels good," he commented. Outside, even though it was evening, it still felt like Death Valley on a bad day.

"Comfort." With a smile Mindy gestured around the temperature-friendly room. "Courtesy of Jason Mallory."

Compliments and gratitude had always embarrassed him. He never knew how to respond and so usually didn't. But in this case it seemed impolite not to say anything.

"Glad to have a hand in making you comfortable." Lord knew one of them should be, he thought. For his part, he felt like a cat on a hot tin roof, unable to stand in one spot, unwilling to jump off.

He looked back at the manila envelope she was holding against her chest. He found himself envying paper. Clearing his throat, he nodded toward the contracts. "I wouldn't ask except that I do need these by tomorrow. I still have to send them to our lawyer."

Rather than feel put-upon, she was happy that he finally seemed to take her seriously about letting her do her job. "Not a problem."

He knew he should be going. He also knew he didn't want to. So instead of heading for the door, he wandered over to the bookcase.

Her taste was eclectic, from a collection of dog-eared Agatha Christie novels to a group of romance novels by a variety of popular authors, past and present, to books on space travel. Lining almost the entire bottom shelf were a number of journalism textbooks. Considering that space was a premium in the tiny apartment, he figured she had to value those a great deal to bring them with her and not just place them in storage somewhere or sell them to a used bookstore.

"Meet with your approval?" she asked after watching him study the titles for a few moments.

"Just curious," he confessed. He turned to look at

her. "Still planning on going into journalism someday?"

All that seemed so far away now, her dreams, her plans for her own future. She shrugged self-consciously in response.

"Maybe. Someday," she echoed. "But not anytime soon."

That didn't sound like the Mindy he was coming to know. She seemed to pursue everything else with zest and enthusiasm. "Why not?"

She placed the envelope on her small table beside the laptop that was perpetually on and shoved her hands into her worn back pockets. "Because right now, the main thing is getting my life in order and some money into a very flat bank account."

It sounded to him as if the divorce settlement wasn't going to be in her favor. He took umbrage at that for her. "If you need a good lawyer—"

She realized that he was talking about her divorce. The subject made her uncomfortable, but she tried to be blasé. "My father said the same thing. So did Nathalie. I'm handling it, thanks."

Truth was, she wasn't handling it. If Brad didn't want to volunteer to pay child support, then she and the babies didn't need his money. At least, not emotionally. She wasn't about to be one of those women who dragged a part of her past into the courtroom, kicking and screaming, just to get vengeance. She didn't need that kind of embarrassment. She would

Silhouette ROMANCE®
DIANA
PALMER
MERCENAR
WOMAN
SOLDIERS OF FORTUNE

much rather just cut her losses and move on with her life.

He knew he should just let it go. Her divorce and its resolution wasn't any business of his. She hadn't asked for his help.

All solid arguments. He didn't listen to any of them. Instead he asked, "How?"

She nodded toward the envelope on the table. "By looking at these contracts for you."

Her tone told him to back away. But there was such a thing as honor, and someone should make note of it. If she couldn't, he could. "He has a moral responsibility to take care of his children, Mindy."

"Brad, it turns out, isn't all that big on morals." And hadn't that been brought home, big-time? "He is, however, very big on getting his own way. I'd just rather put it all behind me, if you don't mind." Much as she hated sending Jason on his way, she wanted to talk about Brad and his impact on her life even less. "Now, if you want these contracts to be ready tomorrow, I suggest that you let me get started on them."

"Right." He took a step toward the door and got no farther. "Mindy..."

She was almost afraid to ask. "Yes?"

"You do know you can talk to me." He turned to look at her. "About anything."

"Anything, huh?" A small smile played with the corners of her mouth. "I've got a cute pair of new shoes I can show you."

She was purposely being evasive. Something he probably would have done in a similar situation. But that didn't mean she could.

"You know what I mean."

"Yes, I know what you mean." She came up to him. Having her so close and yet no closer made his chest ache. He was going to have to work on that, he thought. "And I'm grateful. Really. It's nice to know that I've got a support system to tap into."

He wanted, he admitted to himself, to be far more than her support system. But this would do for now.

He went to open the door and then paused. "Oh, one more thing."

"Yes?"

When she cocked her head and looked at him like that, it was all he could do not to take her face between his hands and kiss her. For all he was worth. This had to be a test of some kind, and he hoped that whoever was keeping tally up there was taking close note.

"How do you feel about coming to the convention in Connecticut with me this weekend?"

She grinned broadly. He trusted her. He finally trusted her to be an asset. Her eyes sparkled as she told him, "I feel great."

"Okay, you handle the details for your trip tomorrow after you get the contracts in."

Doing a little impromptu victory dance wasn't very professional, but she certainly felt like it. "Count on it."

Big mistake a not-so-small voice told him as he left. It was the same voice he recalled hearing in high school when he'd toyed with the idea of asking her out.

This time he chose not to listen to it.

Chapter Nine

After Jason left last night, Mindy found that she was so excited, she could hardly sleep. But morning for once didn't find her dragging, despite her by now traditional bout of morning sickness. Jason's show of faith in her buoyed her spirits to new heights, even for her.

She'd gotten on the phone first thing when she came into the office to make the arrangements, booking two tickets to Hartford, Connecticut, and two rooms at the Hyatt Hotel which was to be at the center of the three-day convention.

When the reservations clerk asked her if she wanted adjoining rooms, she'd hesitated a moment, then said yes. It would make things easier if Jason wanted to work late for some reason.

The surge of energy that went through her was incredible. This was her first business trip. Even though she was going as an assistant who would undoubtedly be in Jason's shadow, it was still a business trip. She was finally a professional.

She knew that in some cases, *business trip* was both a euphemism and an opportunity, focused directly on sex. Any female Brad brought with him, she now knew, was slated to wind up in his bed. Which was why he'd never taken her to any of the insurance conventions he attended or claimed to have attended over the duration of their marriage. She would have cramped his style immensely.

But Jason wasn't like that. She knew she had nothing to worry about. If he said it was a business trip, then the only business they were going to be concerned with, no matter what the hour, was the kind that made the company run. Not what might make her run around a bed.

Not that she would run, she thought with a smile.

If Jason made any overtures toward her, she'd be there for the entire performance until the final curtain came down.

She'd made one mistake marrying Brad and although she had to admit that the thought of a commitment of any kind frightened her now, the thought of doing something equally as stupid by not making herself available to Jason under certain circumstances was just as frightening. She already knew that she and Jason had chemistry. Enough chemistry, she thought remembering their kiss, to blow up a high school chem lab and all the surrounding land.

That might not be enough for a lifetime commitment, but it could certainly lead to a wonderful interlude.

Mindy sighed as she dragged her hand through her hair and looked into the mirror in the ladies' room. She hadn't taken this position with the idea of making it a permanent way of life. Just something to see her through the first year or so of this new odyssey she found herself on. So if she and the boss wound up involved and then eventually going their separate ways, she could handle it. She was a big girl now, she could move on.

Hadn't she proven that to herself already? She was tough, she was empowered....

And then she laughed at herself. "Big words for a rabbit," she said to the wide-eyed woman looking back at her in the mirror.

"Who are you talking to?"

Mindy's heart jumped into her throat as Nathalie stepped out of a stall and headed for the sink.

Mindy thanked God she hadn't said anything else out loud.

"Myself," she mumbled. As an afterthought she nodded toward the mirror. "Bad-hair day."

Nathalie cast a critical eye at Mindy's hair. As always, it was long and sleek, falling about her shoulders like velvet. "My *best* day doesn't look that good," she said with a sigh.

''I like your hair,'' Mindy told her. She turned from the mirror, feeling a little silly at being caught talking to herself. She was also curious now that she thought of it. She would have thought that the logical choice to go to the convention with him would have been Nathalie. ''Jason asked me to go with him to the Hartford convention.''

''Really?'' Nathalie shook the water from her hands and went to pull down a paper towel. She faced Mindy as she slowly dried her hands, amusement playing on her lips. ''Good for him.''

Mindy turned from the sink and studied the older woman to see if she was being sarcastic. She wasn't. ''You're okay with that?''

''I am splendid with that.'' She tossed the paper towel into the garbage. ''Why?'' She paused, looking at Mindy's expression, trying to read it. ''You don't think we're—'' As the thought struck her, she laughed. ''Oh God, I love Jason like a brother, but he's a little too straitlaced to be my type.''

Mindy flushed, realizing that the other woman thought she was asking if they were involved.

''Oh, no. No,'' she repeated with heated emphasis, ''I didn't mean that. I was just wondering why you weren't going with him.'' As his partner, Nathalie seemed like the logical choice.

Nathalie raised a slim shoulder, then let it drop carelessly. ''Someone needs to hold down the fort. Besides,'' Nathalie deliberately lowered her voice even though there was no one else in the restroom,

''I have plans of my own this weekend that have nothing to do with Connecticut, stocks and bonds or hotel food.'' She winked broadly. ''It's not only man who doesn't live on bread alone.''

Nathalie was positively glowing, Mindy thought. ''So it's serious with you and Paolo?''

Nathalie's low, throaty laugh echoed in the room. ''Honey, I'm always serious—up to a point,'' she clarified. ''Some people weren't meant to be married. I found that out after two divorces.'' Nathalie looked at her pointedly. ''However, some people were *born* to be married.''

Mindy nodded. She knew exactly what Nathalie meant. ''Like my parents.''

Nathalie shook her head. ''Don't know them. Do know you.''

That surprised her. ''Me?'' The thought of getting married again gave her goose bumps, and they weren't the good variety. She was quick to set Nathalie straight. ''Oh, no, it's going to be a long time, if ever, before I even *think* of stepping into that arena again. I learned my lesson with Brad.''

Nathalie slipped an arm around the younger woman, giving her a little hug. ''The only lesson you should have learned there is that going with a womanizer can be pretty dicey. Honey, you have 'married lady' written all over you.''

Mindy took that the only way she could and looked down at her waist.

"Am I starting to show?" God, she hoped not. At least, not until this weekend was over.

"Only on your face." Taking her chin in her hand, Nathalie turned Mindy's face toward the mirror to illustrate her point. "You are positively beaming this morning."

Mindy drew her head back. She pointed toward the ceiling. "That's the high wattage from the fluorescent lighting."

"If it was pitch-black in here, you'd be sending out rays. I knew Jason had asked you to go to the convention before you said a word."

Mindy made the logical assumption, even though Jason wasn't due to come into the office until after twelve. He was seeing the CEO at Avalon Avionics this morning. "Jason told you?"

"No, your face told me." Nathalie paused. "You know, Jason is really a great guy. He deserves a little happiness himself. As do you," she emphasized. Looking into the mirror again, she slipped her fingers to the sides of her hair, trying to raise it up a little. "Right now, he's a little soured on marriage, too, but nothing a great girl couldn't change." She turned toward Mindy again. "For my money, I'm betting that girl is you. And I am seldom wrong." She was emphatic about that. "Jason reads the market, I read people," she added for good measure.

"Why is Jason soured on marriage?"

"He didn't tell you?"

"No."

"Then maybe you should ask him."

"He won't tell me." Mindy was surprised that Nathalie would assume that he would. After all, the woman had to know him better than she did. "Jason makes a clam look chatty when he wants to."

Nathalie smiled knowingly. "Clams can be pried open. You get your best pearls that way."

But pearls took a long time to form and she didn't want to wait. "Nathalie, please."

Unable to ignore the entreating look in Mindy's eyes, Nathalie gave in. "He was married to a little nut job while he was going to Columbia for his M.B.A. A debutante who wasn't used to hearing the word no. She chased him all over the place and then when she finally caught him, she lost interest. She started seeing other men behind Jason's back. Did a hell of a number on his pride and his ego."

"Wow, I didn't realize we had that much in common." So, Jason had a cheating spouse, too. Funny how he'd never said anything. Mindy was grateful to Nathalie for telling her.

Nathalie nodded. "Into each life a little scum must fall. Doesn't mean you should let that stain you permanently. This is just between us, understand?"

Mindy nodded.

Nathalie began to head for the door. "Have fun this weekend." Her smile was positively wicked as she added, "And make sure you don't use up your best moves on the convention floor."

She didn't want her other boss getting the wrong idea. "Nathalie, I'm pregnant."

"Well, at least you don't have to worry about what to do about birth control now, do you?" Nathalie laughed at her own wit, then patted Mindy's shoulder. "It's going to be great," she promised just before she walked out of the ladies' room.

"Easy for you to say," Mindy murmured under her breath. Too bad she wasn't that sure herself.

But Nathalie was right. It *was* great. Every second was great, from the moment they disembarked from the chauffeured plane, it promised to be a wonderful experience. She could just feel it in every single fiber of her being.

Like a child on her first major excursion, Mindy sat on the edge of her seat, taking in the sights as the cab made its way through the streets of Hartford to the popular Hyatt Hotel.

Her mood was infectious. Jason felt he would have had to be an alien from another planet not to be at least a little affected. He found himself smiling watching her. If they came to a sudden stop, she gave every indication of being able to pop right through the roof.

"You look like a spring about to be released."

Mindy glanced at him, taking no offense. "Can't help it. This is the first time I've been anywhere in…I can't even remember when."

She might be working this weekend, but it was more like a vacation to her. There were dresses packed in her suitcase that she hadn't had out of the closet since she'd purchased them. She'd tried on each and every one of them to make sure they still fit. Miraculously they did. All she wanted was not to have her waist thicken for just three more days. After that, she could mushroom out and she wouldn't care.

Three more days, that was all she wanted.

She made it sound as if she'd spent the last few years in a cloister. "Didn't you and your husband go on vacations?"

Looking back through the passenger window she shook her head.

"He claimed he was always working, that he always had to stay on top of things. I didn't realize until later that what he had to stay on top of was his current girlfriend of the month." Glancing at him over her shoulder, she flashed a grin in Jason's direction. "Hard to believe that anyone could have been that naive, isn't it?" She called a spade a spade. "Or that stupid."

"The two are not synonymous," he told her. "And I think a certain amount of naiveté is rather sweet."

Because the cab was old and its air-conditioning nonexistent, the windows were opened, letting in the heat from the city. Nonetheless, the small space they were in felt somehow intimate to him. Jason found himself wanting to touch her face, to kiss her.

The urge took on greater proportions, and he almost gave in to it.

But then they were in front of the hotel and the cab

was stopping. It was time to get out. The opportunity passed. He took a deep breath, collecting himself. He was here on business, nothing more.

The doorman opened the passenger door on Mindy's side. By the time she got out, Jason was beside her. The luggage they'd brought with them was on a baggage dolly, following them into the deliciously cool interior of the luxurious hotel.

Mindy felt a little like Cinderella.

"Got the schedule?" he asked her after they had signed in.

She didn't even hesitate. She pulled the single sheet out of the travel bag she'd kept with her all through the flight and held it up.

"Right here." Though she knew it almost verbatim, she still scanned the page with its single-spaced lines. "I'm not sure if I've allotted time to breathe."

"I'll pencil it in," he deadpanned.

Beginning at one o'clock, there was a full agenda ahead of them. Mindy had arranged for him to touch base with a number of senior CEOs for several high-tech and drug companies as well as with two new potential major clients, who were debating signing Mallory and Dixon on as advisors for their companies' IRA portfolios.

"Okay." Jason folded the sheet and slipped it into the pocket of the sports jacket he wore. The tie he'd put on earlier was now stuffed into the other pocket, a tribute to the muggy weather. "We'll stop at the rooms, spend a few minutes settling and then get started—unless you need more time.''

She was grateful for his consideration and just as determined not to need it.

''No more than you,'' she countered. ''I'm still a little unclear what you want me to do,'' Mindy admitted as she hurried alongside him to the first bank of elevators.

Looking around, she noted that the lobby seemed to be teeming with a huge number of people. Were they all here for the convention?

He slipped an arm about her shoulders to keep her from being run over by three children who were chasing each other, weaving in and out of the forest of adults they found themselves in.

''Be charming.''

She tried to decide if he was being serious. ''You want me to be eye candy?''

He found the term insulting and it was hardly what he meant. ''Eye candy doesn't talk. I expect you to talk. To be Mindy.''

She was still having trouble understanding this. ''And this helps how?''

It amazed him how different she was from the girl he'd thought she was. She was completely unassuming, completely unaware of the kind of power she had over people. Over men. Had to be the work of that jackass she'd been married to, he decided. ''Well, if it goes according to plan, you being yourself should make them relax, be more receptive to what I have to say."

She raised her eyes to his, sending an intense ripple through his gut. He tried to remember the last time he ate, blaming his state on the lack of food. "Do I make you relax and be more receptive?"

He looked at her just before the elevator opened its doors, signaling its arrival with a distinct *ding.* "You'd be surprised."

The elevator filled up immediately with people pouring into it from all sides. In less than a heartbeat, there was only enough room left to accommodate a person and a half.

Jason looked down at her. "Do you want to wait?"

She could see the area filling up behind them again. "No, this is fine." Stepping into the crammed car, Mindy pulled him in behind her.

It was a snug fit but not one he was going to complain about. She felt incredibly good against the contours of his body.

Jason found it difficult to keep his mind on the reason they had come to Hartford in the first place.

"You look a little tired." Jason leaned his head down against her ear as he made the observation.

He was escorting her from the hotel's main dining area. They had just spent the past two hours in the company of James Wrinkle, the rising young darling of American Technologies. As evenings went, it had been a very successful one. Mindy, as hoped for, had charmed the pants off the dynamic executive. So much so that at one point Jason had found himself smothering a spike of jealousy. It still amazed him.

He watched her profile. ''Do you want to call it a night?''

It was midnight, two hours past what had become, boringly, her bedtime. Ever since she'd gotten pregnant, her energy level had fallen somewhere into the basement. Something she prayed was just a passing thing.

But she wasn't about to admit that to Jason. The last way she wanted him to think of her was boring.

So she summoned what auxiliary energy she had and cheerfully announced, ''Not if there's some unfinished business.''

There was. All evening he'd felt as if there was, but it wasn't the kind of business she was referring to. It was something he had to work out for himself. He knew what kind of womanizer her ex-husband was. There was no way he wanted her to think of him in the same light.

''We've seen everyone we were supposed to see today. Tomorrow's agenda is pretty full.'' He steered her toward the elevators. Even at this time of night the lobby was more than half-full. It seemed that conventioneers never slept. ''Why don't I take you up to your room so you can get some rest?''

He made it sound as if he was going to deposit her, then leave. ''What are you going to do?''

There was a dimly lit bar just to the left of the last

elevator bank. "I thought I'd get a nightcap before I turned in."

Suddenly she felt a resurgence of energy. "I could join you."

He looked at her uncertainly. "Aren't you not supposed to drink when you're..." Not wanting to embarrass her, he let his voice trail off.

She had no intention of having hard liquor. "I'm assuming a cosmopolitan place like the Hyatt serves ginger ale."

He stopped. "Are you sure you don't want to go to bed?"

The woman who was just then walking by them spared Jason a long, inviting look. It was obvious that she liked what she saw. "If she doesn't want to, handsome, I will."

Mindy tossed her hair over her shoulder, lacing her arms through his possessively. Her smile was wide and dismissing. "Sorry, he's spoken for."

Jason allowed himself to be led off. He looked at her, amused, reminded a little of the old Mindy. "What was that all about?"

She was the face of innocence. "Don't you know a rescue when you see one?"

He laughed. It felt good to relax with her. "Was that what that was?"

"Sure. Unless, of course," she pretended to hedge, "you don't want to be rescued." Mindy glanced toward the departing woman, watching the way her hips swayed beneath the sequined black dress. "She was rather pretty in a surfacy sort of way."

"Was she?" he deadpanned. "I didn't notice." And then his tone grew more serious as he looked at her. "People tend not to notice flashlights when they're standing in the center of a floodlight."

Mindy felt her heart quicken in her chest. "I think that has to be one of the nicest things anyone ever said to me."

"It can't be."

"I'm considering the source. Now, as I recall—" she began steering him toward the bar "—you were going to buy me a ginger ale."

The din in the hotel bar made it difficult to hear. She discovered that she had to watch Jason's lips intently to know what he was saying. Not a hardship. She liked watching them. Liked the way they curved when he gave in to impulse and smiled ever so slightly.

When Jason accompanied her to her room half an hour later, she more than half hoped that he'd find an excuse to come in.

But he didn't.

He waited long enough for her to open her door, and then he bade her good-night.

It took her a long time to fall asleep that night.

It took Jason longer.

Chapter Ten

Jason smiled with satisfaction and relief as he watched his last appointment of the day disappear behind closing elevator doors.

It had been an amazing day, even topping yesterday. To date, this had to be the most successful convention he'd ever attended. He'd seen all the CEOs on his list, talking to them about the future of their respective companies, and had gotten together with all the prospective clients he'd arranged to meet. In both cases there'd been no last-minute cancellations, no apologies extended via phone messages to be collected at a later hour.

The convention had been nothing short of a stellar success, and he wasn't vain enough to attribute that solely to his own abilities. A large part of the credit for captivating his audience rested with Mindy. People were always more receptive when they were in a congenial mood, and Mindy created such a mood by her very presence. She was friendly, warm, funny and intelligent. And if she were any easier on the eye, it might have been against the law.

They made a tremendous team, he thought, and wondered if she felt the same way.

Turning for the elevator, he looked at her. Her midnight-black hair fell freely about her shoulders, making her look like a cross between sheer innocence and a temptress.

What tipped the scales toward the latter was the red dress she wore. A simple sleeveless cocktail dress with a scoop neck, it came in at her waist and then flared, ever so gently, about her hips. It brought attention to her long legs as it stopped inches above her knees.

It seemed guaranteed to bring him to his.

He slipped an arm around her shoulders, guiding Mindy to the side away from the elevators. He had an almost insurmountable urge to kiss her. He'd been fighting that urge for most of the day.

"Well, I'd say that this calls for a celebration. We've gotten all the companies we set out to get to sign on with us."

His enthusiasm was catching. Until yesterday, she'd never seen him in action before. The scope of his knowledge left her in awe. His enthusiasm also made her feel a little heady. ‘‘Doesn’t that usually happen?’’

He thought of the meetings he’d attended with Nathalie. ‘‘Some display a slight reluctance, others like to take a little time to think it over. I’ve never seen all of them ready to jump on the bandwagon this quickly before.’’ Certainly never without Nathalie working her magic.

Mindy wondered if he had any idea how good he was, how much he commanded attention once he got rolling. ‘‘Just goes to show how impressed they are with your wealth of knowledge and your track record.’’

He saw the way several men looked at her as they walked by. That had been going on all day. ‘‘I kind of think it has something to do with your red dress.’’

As if unaware of what she had on, Mindy glanced down at her outfit, then back up at him. ‘‘Excuse me?’’

He tried to memorize every nuance of her face as she spoke. How could her ex have just allowed her to slip through his fingers like that? How could the man have risked losing her by having affairs when he had this at home, waiting for him?

‘‘So far all the head honchos we’ve seen have been men. And you are very much a female.’’

He simply was not giving credit where it was due, she thought. She’d come to realize that was so like him. ‘‘They wouldn’t sign on just because they like the way I look in a red dress.’’

"No, but they wouldn't not sign on, either," he said, "and my guess is that being in your company erased any of the hesitation they might have experienced. You put them at ease, Mindy. Made my job a lot easier."

She was trying to follow what he was telling her. "So I was right? I'm eye candy?"

He went with the image. "Eye candy, ear candy, candy for the soul. You're just as charming as Nathalie said you'd be."

Something fell into place in her head. "Nathalie put you up to this?"

He heard an odd note in her voice. Had he accidentally insulted her by being honest? "Nathalie suggested that I take you in her place, when she couldn't go."

The conversation earlier in the week in the ladies' room replayed itself in her head. Apparently Nathalie wasn't nearly as clairvoyant as she'd begun to think. "But she told you I'd be—" she hunted for the word she assumed he was going for "—charming."

He watched her face, trying to decide whether she was angry or not. "Yes."

"And you had no desire to take me along until she said that." It wasn't exactly a question, more of a hurt assumption.

The corners of his mouth curved slightly. "Let's not mix the word *desire* into this, Mindy."

"Why?"

"Because then we get into a whole different ball game."

Some of the hurt began to fade. She'd seen something in his eyes, something that made her skin warm. Or maybe she was still working on the word *desire.* "What kind of a ball game?"

Was it his imagination, or could he still detect her perfume after all this time? It seemed to be filling his head even as he stood here talking to her. Wanting her.

"The kind where the pitches are a lot wilder than they have a right to be."

Mindy felt as if her heart had suddenly stopped beating. "Such as?"

There was no point in continuing this line of conversation. He was only torturing himself. "Why don't we just have a late dinner for now?"

For now.

Did that mean that this conversation, or this line of thinking would be revisited? Or was she just reading too much into what Jason had just said?

She didn't know if she was high on the moment or from just being here with him. It had been an incredible two days. Accompanying him, having him draw her into the conversation to make her feel as if they were a team, had put a completely different spin on things for her. She felt vital, necessary. Being with Brad had never made her feel as if she had something to contribute. Just the opposite.

As if in response to his question, her stomach rumbled. She smiled, realizing that she wasn't embarrassed. She'd begun to feel far more at ease with him than she had initially.

"Sounds good to me." She thought of putting on something pretty for him. Something sexy and slinky, while she still could, before her figure forbade it. "Maybe I should go upstairs and change."

But he took her arm to prevent her from going anywhere. "Not a hair," he warned her. "I'm pretty much a fan of that dress of yours, too."

It hugged curves on her the way he wished he could. Looking at her now, Jason found it difficult to believe that she was pregnant, certainly not with twins. But he'd heard of women looking almost slender practically to their delivery date. Maybe she fell into that category. She certainly did right now.

She'd selected all her clothes for the trip with him in mind. She'd wanted Jason to notice her before there was too much of her to notice.

"Too bad I'm not going to be able to wear it much longer." A rueful smile played on her lips. "Probably not even until Monday."

"Monday?" He looked at her, confused. "What's Monday?"

"Nothing." She debated explaining. He'd probably think she was crazy. But he was still waiting, so she took a chance and told him. "I just made a deal with God that if He let me fit into all the clothes I packed for this convention, I wouldn't bother Him with anything else. At least for a while."

Amusement highlighted his features. ''And He said yes?''

She deliberately turned around in a circle before him. ''You tell me.''

He almost couldn't. Just looking at her, Jason felt as if he was in danger of swallowing his own tongue. No one should have a right to look as good as she did. His eyes smiled at her.

''I guess He did at that.'' He thought of the celebration he'd suggested to her. He needed someplace public, preferably someplace loud so he couldn't say anything he was going to regret. ''Are you hungry?''

She hadn't eaten all day. There had been trays of appetizers of every variety in the array of hospitality suites they had visited, but her stomach had been giving her too much grief for her to risk trying to keep something down. Until now. Now she suddenly felt as if she was on the edge of almost starving.

''I could eat a horse. A small one,'' she qualified.

He laughed and took her arm, tucking it through his. ''We'll see what we can do about that.''

Jason guided her toward the Empire Room, the most expensive restaurant the Hyatt had. Mindy hesitated at the entrance, looking at Jason. ''We could go somewhere less expensive.''

Right now he would have flown her to Paris if he'd had a private plane at his disposal. He lowered his head and whispered against her ear. ''Don't worry about money.''

His breath rippled all through her, sending out a

squadron of goose bumps all over. It took her a second to regain control. ''But I'm in charge of the budget.''

She really did take her job to heart, he thought. He wondered if she had any idea how much money they had just brought into the fold with the new clients she had help land.

''Relax, we'll make it up on the paper clips and toner,'' he promised. Jason nodded at the maître d' who proceeded to pick up two menus and then motioned for them to follow him into the restaurant. ''I had no idea you were so vigilant.''

He was laughing at her, she thought, but she didn't mind. She felt too good right now to mind. ''I just want to do a good job.''

The maître d' brought them to a table and helped Mindy with her chair.

''The boss highly approves of the job you've been doing,'' Jason told her significantly.

Her eyes met his over the top of her burgundy menu. ''Does he?''

''You have to ask?''

She opened her menu, but the words just swam in front of her. Her attention belonged to the man sitting opposite her. ''Actually, yes. Sometimes it's hard to tell. For instance, I got the impression that the boss wanted me to quit the first day I came.''

Jason paused as a server came by to take their orders for drinks. He had a basic scotch and soda while Mindy ordered a virgin Mary.

"He did," Jason told her the moment the server walked away.

Though she'd suspected it, the admission surprised her. "Why?"

There was noise all around them, but it felt as if their little portion of the restaurant had slipped into an envelope filled with silence. "Because he was afraid that things wouldn't work out."

She made a guess. "Because he thought I was a pampered, spoiled brat?"

His eyes held hers for a long moment, remembering. "No, because he recalled how much he liked you in high school." He paused. "And because he was in a bad place at the time."

Mindy heard only one thing. "He liked me in high school?"

The server arrived, placing the drinks before them. "Couldn't you tell?"

"No—" she lowered her voice "—I thought he didn't know I existed."

They quickly gave their orders to the server, then surrendered their menus.

Jason looked at her after taking a sip of his drink. "People in third-world countries knew you existed, Mindy. You had that kind of aura about you." He smiled. "You still do."

She took a long sip of her drink, as if the seasoned tomato juice could somehow give her the courage to ask the next question. "Then why didn't he ask me out?"

Jason shrugged. It all seemed like such a long time ago. ''Maybe he didn't want to be rejected.''

She curbed the urge to place her hand on his. But her voice touched him. ''He wouldn't have been.''

Jason found that hard to believe. ''All those guys around you—''

''Never meant a thing.''

He laughed shortly. Maybe he remembered things more clearly than she did. ''How about Terry Malone?''

She hardly remembered the teenager he named, her so-called boyfriend at the time. They'd exchanged exactly one letter after they both went away to college, and that was it.

''Just a crush at first. Then I didn't want to hurt his feelings.'' She looked at Jason intently. ''I gave you my book to sign. Why didn't you say anything then?''

''I did.'' He recalled every second of that. ''I said 'Have a nice life.'''

''No, I meant to me.'' Maybe her life would have turned out differently if she'd felt he even noticed her. If she had a clue that he felt something. ''Why didn't you ask me out then? I wanted you to.''

He felt uncomfortable talking about his feelings, he always did. And there was no use in going over the past. ''I'm not very good at reading people. That's why I brought you along to the convention.''

She felt him withdrawing, and she didn't want the subject terminated, didn't want them going back to their corners, business as usual, after what she'd just learned. "Is that the only reason?"

He was honest with her. "It's the reason I gave myself."

She took a deep breath and forged ahead. "And were you lying?"

He debated for a moment. He'd never been one to expose himself emotionally. Risks were for other men to take, not him. Not of this nature.

But there was something in her eyes that wouldn't allow him to withdraw. "Yes."

She smiled, widely. "I never thought I'd be attracted to a liar." She bit her lip. This waltz they were dancing was new to her. Had she made him uncomfortable with the admission. "Or am I not supposed to say that?"

The server arrived, placing their meals before them. He withdrew as unobtrusively as he'd arrived. Jason made a mental note to leave the man a larger tip than he'd planned. "That depends."

She was incredibly aware of her own breathing. And the throbbing of her pulse. "On?"

He looked into her eyes. "Whether you're the one lying now or not."

"Not."

Their own silence hung between them as they began to eat. Mindy had no idea what she was consuming, only that she was going through the motions of chewing, her brain trying to digest this bombshell that had been dropped in her lap. Jason had cared for her.

Might still care for her. The possibilities were as exciting as they were frightening.

What are you doing? You're a pregnant woman, for heaven sakes, not exactly a temptress where the average man is concerned.

But that was exactly it. Jason wasn't the average man. He was Jason, someone who, if she were being honest with herself, had existed all these years on the outskirts of her mind, to be drawn out and thought about when times were practically lonely for her, when Brad was away and she suspected that his business was personal rather than insurance. Jason had always made her pulse kick up a notch, if not race altogether.

As if someone had snapped their fingers, she became aware that there was music playing. She moved her plate back. "Do you dance?"

The question had come out of nowhere, interrupting his thoughts. He'd taken refuge in the constant din of the diners around them, pretending to concentrate on a meal that he had no recollection of eating, even though it was half-gone from his plate.

"I won't step on your toes," he told her.

She wanted to dance. More specifically, she wanted to be in his arms where there was no risk that she'd do something foolish. Right now she felt very vulnerable and just wanted to feel his warmth, to lose herself in the scent of him. What safer place than a small dance floor in a crowded restaurant filled with people?

"I wouldn't say anything if you did."

If this were one of those old campy science fiction series, a robot would be running out, crying, "Danger, Will Robinson, danger." But even if he did, Jason thought, he wouldn't have paid attention. His attention was focused elsewhere.

"I guess you just made me an offer I can't refuse." Rising, he put his hand out to her. Telling himself that he could satisfy this crying need within himself by just holding her to him. By just smelling her hair and touching her hand.

But it wasn't enough.

Holding her like this, swaying with her on a dance floor that seemed to be reserved only for them, wasn't nearly enough. It just made him want her more. "Is this all right?" he asked her.

She leaned her cheek against his chest. "It's perfect."

"The swaying doesn't make you nauseous, does it?" He felt her response. Her light laughter rippled against his chest, cutting through the layers of clothing and going straight into the heart of him.

After a moment she raised her head and looked at him. "How long were you married?"

The question surprised him. He didn't recall telling her that he'd married. "How did you know? Do I dance married?"

She laughed. "No, and before you ask, I'm not that intuitive. Nor did I snoop. Nathalie told me."

He granted the fact that there were times when he

could be very dense. But even he was beginning to get the impression that Nathalie was playing God again, arranging things on life's chessboard. "Nathalie seems to be taking a lot of liberties these days."

She wasn't going to go there. "No sidetracking. How long were you married?"

"Six years." The music was soft, stirring. It went with the atmosphere. With the company he was keeping. "Unless you want to know how long I was happily married. Then it's about ten minutes."

An instant camaraderie sprang up within her. How long had she suspected that she was in a bad union before she actually allowed herself to admit it?

"Could have been worse," Jason allowed philosophically. "I'm not sure how, but things can always be worse." Time to turn the tables, he thought. "How long were you married?"

"Almost seven years." In some ways it felt like forever, in others, as if it had never even happened. At least it was all behind her. "I kept telling myself I had the perfect marriage."

He thought of the little she'd let on and what Nathalie had told him. He knew all about men like Brad. Image-conscious egomaniacs.

"Even though he wanted you to be Donna Reed?" She looked at him quizzically. "You know, vacuuming the living room in high heels and pearls. Looking perfect." His eyes swept over her. *Perfect,* that was the word for her. "You probably had the 'perfect' part down pat."

When he said it like that, it all fell into place. God, she'd been such a fool. "He had a game plan, all right. Unfortunately, it was from the early sixties." Without realizing it, she leaned her cheek a little closer against him. "I should have put my foot down."

He didn't want her feeling like a fool. These kinds of things happened to everyone. To him as well as her. Once he'd let Debra into his heart, he'd found himself in love with her. And stunned at the way she rebuffed him. There was no explaining people like Brad and Debra, there was only an understanding for their own motives, his and Mindy's, in reacting the way they had.

"You loved him. Love makes you forgive a lot of things."

She looked at him, surprised at how well he understood. "Yes, I loved him. In hindsight, a lot more than he loved me, I guess."

He wondered if there was any chance at all of a reconciliation. If the man said the right words, would she let him come back into her life? Did she still love him? He didn't want to know the answer to the last question, but at the same time he did. "Have you spoken to him since you moved out here?"

"No." Although she knew she was going to have to. Brad deserved to know he was going to be the father of twins. But it was something she kept putting off until she felt up to it, up to hearing his voice and not wanting to shout at him.

Jason's hand tightened around hers. "Good."

She raised her head to look at him. His response surprised her. And filled her with a warmth that had nothing to do with the state of the air-conditioning in the restaurant.

She smiled at him.

There went his gut again, he thought. Tightening like a dry-clean-only sweater thrown into a dryer. He glanced over to their table, to the half-eaten portions still sitting there. "Are you still hungry?"

Not for food she wasn't.

Getting a grip on herself, Mindy shook her head. "No, you?"

"No." He took her hand, leading her from the floor. They stopped at the table for her to get her purse. Jason settled the account, left a generous tip and took her hand again.

He guided her to the elevator bank closest to the restaurant. "It's late."

Did that mean he was sending her off to her room? Or was he just searching for something to say? She glanced at her watch. She didn't want the evening to end just yet. "It must be early somewhere in the world."

"Must be," he echoed.

But it was late here, and he had to keep that in mind. Just as he had to keep in mind that what he was feeling had no place in either of their lives right now. She was pregnant, he was her boss, and they had both been badly burned by the people they'd chosen to spend their lives with. Not exactly great odds for starting a new relationship.

The elevator car that opened before them was empty. They got in. There was no excuse for him to stand so close to her, but he did anyway.

Mindy closed her eyes, letting her senses drift. Letting her mind do the same. Both took her to places she was afraid she might never be allowed to reach in reality.

''Well, this is our floor,'' Jason said needlessly when the doors opened on twelve. He felt her reluctance to leave. It matched his own. ''We could always go for a longer ride if you want.''

She laughed. They could ride up and down the elevator like a couple of kids on a holiday. But they weren't a couple of kids. They were adults now, with more responsibilities than seemed fair. She shook her head, stepping out. ''No, getting out here will be fine.''

They walked to their adjoining suites, his arm tucked in through hers protectively.

Mindy felt her knees becoming less than solid. She didn't want the evening to end, didn't want him to say good-night at her door and turn to go to his. Her mind scrambled for a reason to make him stay.

''Would you like to come in?'' Mindy turned from the door she'd just unlocked. ''For an incredibly small bag of salted nuts, or volume-challenged little drinks, or whatever it is they stock in that tiny little refrigerator in the corner of my room?''

He didn't want anything that he could find in the suite besides her. "I shouldn't."

"You're the boss. You can do anything you want."

That was just the problem, he was her boss, and because he was, he couldn't do anything he wanted. "It's not that easy."

She refused to give up. "It is if you say it is."

Her words were seducing him and he found that his resistance was falling into the basement. "I'm not the only one involved here."

"No," she agreed looking at him significantly, "you're not."

Everything within him begged him to take her into his arms. Only his mind was the last holdout and it was sinking fast. "Mindy, you're making this very difficult."

She rose on her toes, her breath playing along his lips as she asked, "Difficult how?"

Was it his imagination, or had the lights in the hall just dimmed? "Difficult to say no."

Mindy placed her hands on his arms. "Then don't say it."

"Mindy..."

"Yes?"

A man was only so strong, had only so much within him to draw on that might be counted on to keep him noble. After that, it was every emotion for itself.

Just as it was now.

Gently threading his fingers through her hair, Jason

cupped the back of her head and tilted her face up toward his.

And kissed her.

The way they both wanted him to.

Chapter Eleven

Mindy didn't remember opening the door that led into her room.

The one that led into her soul was another matter.

Within a heartbeat of falling headlong into Jason's kiss—a kiss that had completely swept over her—Mindy became vaguely aware that they had somehow managed to get into her room. Somehow managed to close the door behind them.

She had no recollection of stepping over the physical threshold, only of stepping over a line she'd known all along was waiting for her to cross. Moving to a space, a place that had been waiting for her ever since she'd seen Jason again.

Longer.

Excitement raced through her as his lips gently assaulted hers. As they worked away the layers of fear, of sanity, of logic, going to the core of her where there was only desire, only passion that had been kept in check for far too long.

With a small cry of exhilaration, she raised herself up on her toes and kissed Jason back, long and hard. Seductively.

Spelling his undeniable undoing.

It was hopeless. If he meant to pull back, to cease before this got into any deeper waters, he'd lost that small opening in time without even realizing that it was there for him. He was swept away on the tidal wave of his own desires as they crashed into hers, melding, forming something that was greater than the sum of its parts.

Greater than the sum of them.

His mouth raced over hers, moving urgently, yet softly to her face. Tasting her skin and finding that he couldn't exist another moment without having her.

Was he crazy?

The question echoed loudly in his brain. Probably was the only answer he could come up with. Sane men didn't do this kind of thing, didn't leave themselves open to being stripped of all their defenses the way he just had.

Sane men didn't ache this way for a dream that had passed.

With the last ounce of strength he had, Jason managed to draw his mouth from hers, managed to separate himself from her, leaving only enough room between them for a prayer.

''Mindy, maybe—''

Her heart hammered so hard, she couldn't quite hear him at first. She read his lips instead. Lips that looked to be as swollen as hers felt.

She could feel fear nibbling away at her happiness and shook her head.

''No, no choices, Jason. No pauses, no thoughts. You can't just reduce me to the consistency of a puddle of spring rainwater and then just pull back for a debate.''

He knew it wasn't her he was doing it to but himself. He framed her face with his hands. Her face had been etched on his brain all these years and would haunt him forever no matter what happened in this room.

''You always have a choice,'' he told her quietly. Even if that choice wound up killing him.

''I know,'' she whispered. ''And I've made it.''

There was surrender in her eyes. It both empowered and humbled him, crumbling the last shreds of any resistance he might have had to offer.

Holding her to him, kissing her lips, her hair, the hollow of her throat, Jason slowly slid the zipper at the back of her dress down to its source.

And then the dress was being held in place only by the press of their warm bodies. He stepped back a fraction of an inch. The dress sank to the floor like a woman swooning in an old-fashioned melodrama.

There was nothing old-fashioned about Mindy.

She was nude from the waist up, a crimson lace thong and thigh-high dark stockings her only cover. She still had on her high heels. Her long dark hair fell against her shoulders, the ends resting seductively above her full breasts.

She was every man's fantasy.

Jason's gut tightened so hard he found he had trouble drawing in a breath.

His gaze warmed her. She felt beautiful, desirable, all the things she hadn't felt for so very long. Ever since Brad had begun to distance himself from her.

She could feel her pulse jumping in anticipation.

Eager, Mindy pushed his jacket off his shoulders, sending it down to the floor beside her dress. She began tugging at his shirt, desperate to have the feel of his skin against hers.

Desperate to have the feel of him.

Her breath shortened, her pulse rate increased. She felt as if none of the last few years had happened. She felt as if Brad had only been a bad dream, a poor substitute for the man she'd fantasized about having in her life. There was no question about it, her ex-husband was a pale imitation of the man who now wanted her.

A man she wanted more than anything in the world.

She had to keep reminding herself to breathe, had to keep reminding herself that she wasn't dreaming, that this was real. That Jason was real. And that this moment existed.

Her eyes on his, she worked the buttons of his shirt loose, then stripped him of it. It landed somewhere in the vicinity of his jacket; she didn't quite know where. Her attention was focused on the belt on his trousers, and she was embarrassed and excited at the same time.

His hands moved hers away, undoing the buckle for her when she fumbled. Her movements became more sure. The small intake of breath as she slid down the zipper came from him, melding with her own.

Excitement rose another notch, sizzling along her very skin.

She could feel herself throbbing, yearning. Growing damp just from the thought of him. And when he placed her hands on his hips, guiding her movements until she'd carefully brought down his trousers and the briefs he had on beneath, she made a small unintelligible sound, as all of her tightened like a spring that had been overwound.

He worked his fingers into the slender bands of her thong, drawing it away from her hips, her thighs, her legs. The stockings seemed to roll away under their own power, coaxed only a little by the palms of his hands.

And then there was nothing left between them except for hopes unrealized.

Somehow, their mouths sealed to each other's, they found themselves beside her bed. And then on it. Each tiny bit of the journey was a mystery to her, to be explored later in the darkness, when she would hug this memory to her breast.

But for now it was to be traversed, experienced. Absorbed. Every fiber in her being throbbed. His hands were everywhere, caressing her, loving her. Making her his. As if there had ever been a question of that.

She pressed her body against his, aching for the heat she felt. Aching for a fulfillment she'd never yet experienced.

Pulses raced, fingers flew, barriers were crossed. Heat rose like a protective shield, encasing them from the world, sealing them to each other.

Over and over again he kissed her, branded her, enflamed her. Jason's hands and lips seemed to be everywhere, creating cataclysms in their wake all along her skin. She twisted and turned as climaxes scrambled over her body, making her anticipate a final release she had yet to ever feel.

Even now her body was being held hostage by sensations the likes of which she'd never known before.

Brad had never been a satisfying lover. In this day and age, she'd still managed to come to him a virgin, never having known another man. Never having known that there could be both patience and excitement in lovemaking, that there was a wealth of sensations waiting for her to experience—most of which she had never even touched upon.

When the first burst upon her suddenly, she arched her body, trying to prolong it, to go with it even as wonder assailed her. Her eyes flew open and she looked at Jason as a moan escaped her lips.

Jason looked at her, confusion creasing his brow. "Did I hurt you?"

She bit her lower lip, shaking her head. Her breath was in short supply, and it took a moment to find any so she could answer.

"No. I just never..."

It was as if her thoughts had also become his. Because he understood what she was trying to tell him. "Never?"

She pressed her lips together. Her whole body was still tingling. "Never."

And then he smiled at her. A soft, generous, kind smile that went straight into her heart.

It was clear now. He knew what he had to do. To give her pleasure the magnitude of which she'd never known. He had no one to compete against, no one's shadow to conquer. Pregnant or not, she'd come to him like a virgin, someone who had never known the pleasures of true lovemaking. It was his responsibility to lead her there with gentleness and sensitivity in attendance.

He set about showing her just how it could be between a man and a woman.

And as he did, she showed him a new world, as well. Mindy was receptive, eager to experience, eager to give back, when she was able, what she had been given.

She was nothing at all like Debra.

Experiencing all this for the first time again through her, Jason felt as if he had been given the most generous gift of all.

He teased, he caressed, he fondled and explored. Each movement seemed to be only a shade more intense than the last, but he played her like an instrument, strumming her strings until they sang, and in so doing he brought her to climax after climax. Each time another one racked her body, she was certain this one was the best, that there couldn't be anything better in its wake.

But there was.

And when she seemed to be on the edge of exhaustion, when her breathing was so audible he was afraid she was going to hyperventilate, Jason poised himself over her. His eyes on hers, their hands touching, he slowly entered, even now ready to pull back if she gave the slightest indication that this felt wrong to her.

He knew he would crumble if he had to stop, but she had made him a generous lover. And there was no indication that she wanted anything but to share this last plateau with him. To scale it together with him and to become one, if only for a crystal moment in time.

He sheathed himself in her. She began to move. He felt her breathing quickening again. Felt her tightening around him. It took everything in him to hold himself in check.

Mindy raised her head from the pillow, seizing his

mouth as their hips locked and began to move in time together.

Faster and faster they went until the end of the race was reached and lights flashed all around them, raining down in a glowing shower.

Exhausted, pleased leagues beyond any barometer's ability to measure, Jason found himself wanting to remain like this forever, joined with her for all time. But reality was there, nudging at him, making him afraid that he was crushing her.

With a reluctance that was almost overwhelming, Jason raised himself on one elbow, all he had the strength for, and looked at her face. She appeared a little dazed and very much like the girl he'd fallen in love with back in high school.

"Are you all right?"

All right? She was so far beyond all right, there were no road maps out here. After a beat, she sighed and then smiled at him. "Listen."

He didn't hear anything. "For what?"

No, he wouldn't hear anything. The sound was only echoing in her head. "I think that's the sound of the twins, cheering."

He laughed, the last of his concern ebbing away. At least for the moment. Rolling off her, he gathered Mindy to him and kissed the top of her head.

The kiss was so gentle, so sweet, it made tears gather in her eyes.

He felt one against his chest as it slid down. Concern returned, driven by a coach with six black horses.

"Mindy?" He looked down at her and saw her eyes. "Are you crying?"

"No, that's just my eye sweating." She wiped the back of her hand against her eyes to get rid of any further evidence, then sighed deeply. She felt as if it came from the bottom of her toes. "I'm not sure I can move. Ever again." She saw the look of concern entering his eyes. "No, no, you didn't hurt me," she told him, second guessing what he was about to say. "Just exhausted me, that's all."

She curled into him, knowing that even now, in this most intimate of situations, she should hold back. But it wasn't in her nature to be secretive, not really. Brad had triggered a fear of verbal intimacy in her until she felt as though they were just two strangers, even when they made love. But Jason had cracked open that door again and she felt grateful, even as she knew she was leaving herself vulnerable, leaving herself exposed to being hurt in the long run.

But all that counted was right now.

She felt she should try to explain. "Whenever we were together like this, Brad never cared about getting me to any destination."

The euphemism amused him. "Destination? Is that what we call it now?"

We.

It had such a beautiful ring to it, she thought. She knew she couldn't allow herself to run through the fields of expectations as yet unvoiced, but part of her felt that there was no harm, as long as she didn't hold him to it, to pretend that they were already there.

She cleared her throat. "I wasn't sure just what to call it, but I thought the word had a nice ring to it." Because he had brought her to a place, a very special place, she'd never been to before, not even briefly.

Yes, it did have a nice ring to it, he thought. And so did making love with her.

Jason turned toward her now, smoothing back her hair from her face, looking at her and berating himself for not having the courage, years ago, to approach her. Again he wondered what turns life would have taken for him if he only had.

"So, I take it that you're not sorry about what we just did?"

"Sorry?" Sorry? When her whole body was singing? When she felt as if she'd just been reborn? How could he even *think* that? "I'll show you how sorry I am." She lifted her head and kissed him with all the passion she could summon.

He felt himself responding to her all over again, as if they just hadn't made love for the past forty-five minutes or so. As if he was still anticipating what it would be like to have her for the first time.

Except that now he knew. And anticipated it all the more.

He laughed, pulling her against him. "Okay, but you asked for this."

Yes, she thought, she had. And then she grinned.

"If I'd known it was this simple, I would have asked a long time ago."

She was kidding. He knew that. And yet, the thought warmed him even as he began to make love with her again.

The feel of the bed moving woke him. In a sleep-induced haze, he was aware of a sudden lack of something beside him. Opening his eyes with the reluctance of one who hated waking in the morning, it took Jason a few moments to get his bearings and orient himself.

He was in a hotel room.

Her hotel room.

And she wasn't beside him. His eyes, already opened, focused as consciousness leaped into his veins, pushing him over the line into complete wakefulness.

He sat up in bed, the sheet curled around his body haphazardly. The comforter missing. He glanced over the side of the bed to see if it had been a casualty of last night's lovemaking, but it wasn't there. Just as he began to wonder where it could have gotten to, he heard a sound, muffled but clearly wretched. It came again. He scrambled to his feet, forgetting about niceties like clothing and hurried to the source.

Mindy was on the other side of the door, wrapped in the missing comforter and on her knees before the toilet bowl. Absolutely miserable.

"Mindy?"

"Go away," she begged. "I don't want you seeing me like this." It was hard to get the words out without giving in to the overwhelming craving of heaving up everything that had been stored in her for the past twenty-four hours.

But rather than get out, he moved forward.

"Go away," she ordered. This time she couldn't hold the urge in check. This time she threw up again, certain as she did it that she was grossing him out.

When she finished purging herself, she was surprised to discover that she wasn't alone in the room. Jason was bending down, a clean, wet cloth in his hand, wiping her cheek.

"Here, you can probably do this better than I can."

She took a deep breath. It was over. For another twenty-four hours, and then it would come again, like rampaging Visigoths, determined to plunder everything from her stomach that she'd eaten in the past day. She sagged against the side of the tub, looking up at him.

"Why are you still here? And why are you not dressed?" Although she had to admit that he looked even better in the light of day than he did in the glow of the artificial light.

"I thought you might need help to get on your feet." He took her hand. "There wasn't time to get formal."

She let him help her up and laughed despite herself. "Thanks. I need to brush my teeth," she murmured.

He nodded, letting go of her hand. "As long as you're all right."

She was better than all right, she thought, watching the way his hips moved as he walked out. She was downright near fabulous.

Jason was very aware of Mindy standing behind him as he settled up their account for the past three days. As he checked them out of paradise and back into the everyday world that they ordinarily inhabited.

It was time, he told himself sternly, waiting for his credit card to be returned to him, to put everything behind him and realize that last night and this morning had been an aberration. That he had done the unthinkable, given in to himself and taken advantage of her at a vulnerable moment.

Words, when there were no stocks-and-bonds issues attached to them, often failed him. They failed him now even as he stood there with his back to her, trying to mentally frame an apology. He hadn't meant to compromise her the way he had, to jeopardize their relationship the way he did just because he couldn't rein himself in.

Just because she was the most beautiful woman he'd ever seen.

So, unable to say it right, he said nothing at all, retreating instead, into verbiage that concerned itself strictly with the real reason they had come here. It was safer that way.

"You did a great job this weekend," he told her

as they stepped outside with their luggage. The hotel valet flagged down a taxi for them. "You should be very proud of yourself. And very busy once we get back to the office."

There were new contracts to issue and company data to input and catalog. Not to mention new stock data that he had culled from his appointments with the various CEOs. All that had to be written up. Mindy had faithfully recorded a great deal of what had been said, both by hand and by tape, but it still needed to be put into their computers so that he could access it at a later date.

He sounded so distant, she thought, as if last night had never happened. As if he hadn't made her feel like a human being instead of a miserable mother-to-be.

But she had to remember that he wasn't exactly going to go skipping through the fields, forgetting their working relationship just because they'd slept together. After all, he wasn't paying her to warm his sheets, he was paying her a good salary to be an asset, and she intended to be one. The greatest one he'd ever had.

And if he was happy at the office, he'd be that much more receptive to her on the home front.

Maybe, she mused as she got into the taxi, this job wasn't just going to be a stepping stone to something else for her. Maybe this *was* something else and she could make a career of it.

A career out of helping Jason. She liked the sound

of that, the feel of it. She was aware that there were certainly far worse ways to go than being the helpmate of a man she loved.

Life felt very, very good and if not in place the way she would have originally wanted it, it was very, very close to it.

Chapter Twelve

Ribbons of nostalgia threaded around her as Mindy sat down in the bright, formal dining room. Ever since she'd returned to New York, each time she walked into her parents' house—the house that, like her parents, had remained like a steadfast beacon through all the years of her life—she would become aware of deep-seated feelings of déjà vu commanding her attention.

It was comforting to know that some things never changed, no matter what cataclysmic events took place in the rest of the world. Or her life.

Her mother always did know how to set a good table, Mindy thought. It was one of the things her mother took pride in, along with a degree in engineering from NYU, awarded in the days when most women didn't get engineering degrees.

For all her education, Marilyn Conway always sounded like her mother rather than the instructor she was at the same college where she had initially gotten her degree. This evening was no exception.

Marilyn peered at her face as she set down the last of the dinner she'd prepared. "So, how's it going? The new job, the china closet you call an apartment, everything okay?"

Mindy tried unsuccessfully not to frown at the questions her mother served her in addition to the weekly dinner she had agreed to as part of the terms for the loan she'd let them give her.

Served her right for not wanting to take the money with no strings attached, she thought. She'd told her parents that she would only accept the money from them if she could pay interest on it. Her mother had turned around and made a counteroffer, saying that what she wanted more than money was the pleasure of her company. Loving her mother and suffering from a bout of amnesia, which caused her to forget just how many questions her mother was able to cram into a minute when she'd been a dating teenager, Mindy had heard herself saying yes.

Regret embraced her decision.

Her father leaned in her direction. His eyes were gray and kind.

"Humor her, Mindy. Interrogation is your mother's only outside hobby. She's gotten rusty since you've been away, with no one but me to practice on.'' Her siblings had all scattered into intense lives of their own. Right now she envied them. ''And we all know what an exciting life I lead.'' Her father was chief accountant for an old, respected institution and looked every inch the part. ''Be patient, it'll get more subtle.''

''Not that I remember,'' Mindy murmured under her breath.

Her mother eyed her. ''If you have something to say, Mindy,'' Marilyn told her briskly as she helped herself to a serving of carrots julienne, ''please share it with the class, not your salad.''

Mindy sighed. You can take the woman out of the classroom, but you can't take the classroom out of the woman. At least, not when it came to her mother. ''The job is going great and I'm almost finished decorating the apartment.''

Marilyn raised an inquisitive eyebrow. ''What's to decorate? You plug in a lamp, hang up a bathroom towel and violà, you're done.''

''Marilyn—'' The reprimand was softly voiced, but carried weight nonetheless. Looking back, Mindy didn't remember ever hearing either one of her parents raise their voices, not even her mother.

Marilyn Conway looked at the man she'd married at nineteen.

''What? I'm just saying that there isn't much to do in an apartment the size of a birdcage.'' The short reprieve was over. Her mother directed her attention back to her. ''Why couldn't you let your father and me lend you more money so you could get something decent?''

Mindy had thought this particular debate was over. Obviously, she underestimated her mother's tenacity. ''It *is* decent, Mother.'' Mindy played her ace card. ''And it's in a good neighborhood.''

It was her mother's turn to frown. Deeply. It was obvious that their definitions of *good* varied by a wide margin.

''Huh. I've heard what they call it. The Girl Ghetto.'' Marilyn gave her a triumphant look, pleased with herself for being in tune with what she took to be the latest hip term. ''Ghetto, that can't be good.''

It wasn't her heightened hormones that made her become defensive, it was the old mother-daughter conflict that had always existed between them, right beside the huge affection they bore for each other. Just because you loved someone, Mindy knew, didn't make you blind to their faults.

Unless that someone was Brad, a small voice whispered. But even there, she'd regained her vision.

''In this case,'' she told her mother, ''it's just an expression.'' She glanced toward her largely silent father as she added, ''And I love my apartment.'' Her father, she'd learned a long time ago, had a survivalist mentality and rarely got in the middle of their ''debates'' unless he deemed it absolutely necessary.

Marilyn buttered her bread a little too briskly. She obviously hated the thought of her daughter living in such sparse accommodations. "You always did have a habit for caring about strays and misfits. Part of your loving nature, I guess." Her eyes narrowed to focus on Mindy's barely touched plate. "You're not eating."

Howard placed his hand over his daughter's, curtailing the response that seemed ready to be fired. "She's eating, Marilyn. You've got enough food there to feed the First Infantry."

The abundance of food on display had apparently nothing to do with it. Marilyn's gaze was accusing as it rested on her daughter. "And she's supposed to be eating for three, not half a munchkin."

Enough was enough. "Mom, I know you mean well, but I'm twenty-eight years old. I learned to eat when I'm hungry a long time ago."

And right now, although everything looked good, Mindy found herself not wanting to eat. Her stomach felt as if it was in a perpetual uproar. She and Jason had been back from the conference for three days, and he was behaving almost as standoffish as he had the first week.

The uneasiness over the reversal in behavior was taking a definite toll on her appetite. Just as her mother was taking a definite toll on her nerves.

Concern colored the older woman's features. "You're not hungry? Are you sick?" She looked at the serving dishes on the table. "Is there something wrong with the food?" She was on her feet even as she made the offer. "I can make you something else if you'd rather not eat any of—"

Mindy made a grab for her mother's wrist before she could get away, tethering her in place. "Mom, Mom, slow down." A smile finally made its appearance as she tried to coax her mother into inactivity. "I'm not here for the food, I'm here for the company, remember?" Still holding her mother's wrist, she looked to her father for help. "Back me up here, Dad."

Howard looked mildly at his more tumultuous spouse. "She's right, you know."

With a mighty sigh, Marilyn sank back down into her chair. Her wrist held prisoner by her daughter's surprisingly strong grip, she didn't have much of a choice. But she wasn't about to surrender entirely. "You'll take some food home with you."

Mindy smiled. "I'll take some food home with me," she agreed.

"Good." And then Marilyn's eyes grew wide as if remembering something. Her tone was almost icy as she said, "Oh, and by the way, not that it matters, but your father made me promise I'd tell you so, I'm telling you—"

A little uneasy, Mindy looked from her father back to her mother. "Tell me what?"

Marilyn's frown was deep, going clear down to the bone. "That...that useless excuse for a human being called here, looking for you."

She knew instantly. Her mother had never cared

for Brad, had never forgiven him for taking her away from the family so abruptly that she hadn't even returned home, just had her things shipped out to Illinois. "Brad? Brad called here? What did he want?"

"You," her father said without ceremony.

Her mother shot a glare over to her father. It clearly stated that she would handle the narrative from here.

"He wanted to talk to you. When I told him you didn't live here, he wanted to know your address and phone number." Marilyn raised her chin proudly in a movement that was echoed time again by her daughter. "I wouldn't give it to him. That decision I'm leaving up to you."

Her mother rarely made those kinds of concessions without haggling over them first. Mindy was touched. "Thank you, Mother."

And then the other shoe dropped. "But if it was mine to make—"

"We already know what you would do, Marilyn," her husband cut in. He looked at Mindy. "Which is why I'm keeping her away from sharp instruments and from the airlines."

Mindy smiled. She knew her mother meant well, as did her father. She could always rely on them for moral support no matter what was happening in her life. But even so, it had been difficult for her to come to them and tell them the drastic turns her life had taken. That she was getting a divorce. It made her feel like a child again, having screwed up royally, even though she knew that the mistakes she'd made had been those of a woman and not that of an adolescent.

Pregnant and single again, who would ever have thought she'd find herself here? Certainly not her.

She pressed her lips together, trying to decide what she was going to do about Brad's latest intrusion into her life. Why was he calling? To apologize? To get even? With Brad, she never knew.

Marilyn looked hurt that the odds were two against one. Especially since she meant well. "I just think he should be taught a lesson, that's all."

"He has," her husband calmly pointed out, looking at his daughter. "Mindy's left him. That should be lesson enough for anyone."

A thought suddenly occurred to her. Mindy looked at her mother, trying not to show her concern. "He's still in Illinois, isn't he? I mean, he hasn't come to New York looking for me, has he?"

To be honest, for the life of her, she couldn't see why he would come after her. When the initial shock of having his ego assaulted because someone deigned to leave him faded, Brad had looked relieved to be able to go back to his flavor-of-the-week girlfriend without the need of making up lame cover-ups for his absence.

Marilyn nodded, her short straight black hair bobbing. "Caller ID had your old number on it." Her disapproval was very evident. "Really, Mindy, I think you should at least get the house."

She'd already made her concessions. "I'm fine

with losing the house, Mom, as long as it means I lose Brad along with it.'' She smiled brightly at her mother. Maybe she would have something to eat after all. It was one way to get her mother off her back. ''Pass the pork chops, please.''

Marilyn smiled as she reached for the large platter in the center of the table and passed it to her daughter.

In another part of Manhattan, Eloise Vale tapped her slim silver pen against the side of the keyboard she'd pushed to the side. Her computer slumbered while her mind raced around in an unrewarding circle.

She wasn't getting anywhere.

The news that the mayor was debating cutting off funding to her foundation had knocked the stuffing out of her.

Eloise pushed herself away from her desk. ''Ain't gonna happen, Billy,'' she murmured under her breath.

She might not be able to solve world hunger, but the fate of her beloved organization was something she could handle. It all depended on her getting the mayor to change his mind. That was where the focus of her main offense lay.

There was no way city funds were going to cease flowing in her direction when the service she was supplying was so vital, she thought fiercely. Bill probably thought it was frivolous. There were times when they were younger that she'd thought Bill incapable of an intelligent reasoning process. After all, it wasn't as if she was attempting to line her own coffers. God knew she'd already sunk a great deal of the money Walter had left her into running Manhattan Multiples. But she certainly couldn't keep up that sort of thing indefinitely. If nothing else, she would eventually run out of money, and there were her own triplets to think of.

She had to stop thinking of them under that label, she admonished herself the second she'd referred to them by the term. They weren't triplets, they were individuals. Carl, John and Henry. Perhaps not as different as night, day and noon, she allowed, but her thirteen-year-old sons all had different personalities and absolutely hated being lumped together like "three peas in a pod," an expression Walter had been so fond of.

Something else to teach mothers-to-be expecting multiple births, she noted mentally. Thinking of the babies as a unit hardly ever proved to be in their best interests.

Looking at the photograph taken of her sons when they were, appropriately enough, three, Eloise sighed, giving herself a private moment. Replacing the photograph on her desk, she rose to her feet.

God generally helped those who helped themselves, she reminded herself.

It was time to start organizing a fund-raiser.

"You're in early."

Jason had come in purposely twenty minutes ahead of his usual time, thinking that he could safely traverse the area from the front door to his office without having to pass her. But there she was, sitting at her desk, petite, lovely and larger than life. Working. He just couldn't get a break, he thought.

Mindy looked up from her computer. Her fingers ceased flying across the keyboard. The radiant smile on her face vividly brought back memories of the weekend they'd spent together.

Of her in bed, in his arms…

Jason caught himself before his thoughts strayed any further.

Made him any warmer.

He looked surprised, Mindy noted to herself. Didn't he expect her to be here this morning? Or was there some reason he was trying to get in early? It couldn't be to avoid talking to her. Could it?

"I didn't have to stop to throw up this morning," she told him, "so I thought I'd come in and complete some of the reports you said you needed on your desk as soon as possible."

He knew he'd said that to her, but it hadn't been an absolute order. Frustrated by the turmoil of what he was feeling, not knowing what to do to put it to rest, he admonished her.

"You know, you don't have to be 'super assistant.' For one thing, we're not paying you enough to knock yourself out like this."

Was that criticism, or was he just looking out for her? She wasn't sure. Mindy tried to put a positive spin on his words. ''Everyone needs a goal. I like to challenge myself to do a little better every day. Keeps it interesting.''

If she extended that to her private life, he thought, it meant that last Sunday night had just been the threshold of what she could do.

Damn it, he had to stop thinking like that.

Last Sunday night had happened because he'd allowed his guard to drop. It wasn't something he intended to have happen again. There was no place in his life for an office romance, even if that romance did include Mindy. He was the reason Debra was dead. How could he allow himself to reach for happiness when she couldn't reach for anything at all?

''Still,'' he told her, ''you don't want to push yourself too much.''

Did that mean he cared and he just didn't know how to show it? The thought that he did warmed her.

Just looking at him warmed her.

In a good way, not the way the sticky heat just beyond the perimeter of the building's air-conditioning system threatened to leave its brand on everyone who ventured outside today.

Trying to divine his meaning, Mindy never took her eyes off his face. ''Don't worry,'' she told him cheerfully, hoping it was infectious, ''I know my own limits and capabilities.'' She wanted to bring an end to the discussion, then remembered the call she'd taken just before Jason had walked in. ''Nathalie called in, said she was running a little late but she'd be here.''

He wasn't feeling very tolerant this morning and he knew it, but there didn't seem to be anything he could do to stop himself. ''More like running around the bed, chasing Paolo.''

Mindy stopped moving things around on her desk and looked at him. ''Don't you approve of love, Jason?''

He snorted. Right now, he sincerely doubted Nathalie would know love if it bit her on the ankle. ''It's not love, it's lust.'' And then he shrugged carelessly. All he wanted to do was retreat to his office, to get away from her line of vision. From those beautiful eyes that were haunting him, even as he stood here. ''But it makes her happy, so, yes, I approve.''

He didn't sound it, Mindy thought. Neither did he sound very understanding—giving such a harsh label to what Nathalie was feeling.

She was being too sensitive, she told herself. Came with the new territory, she supposed. But there were times when she was certain that Jason attempted to distance himself from her.

It had been more than three days since they'd returned to New York, and he hadn't once suggested going out for coffee or dinner.

Or anything.

She bit her lip, trying not to be petulant. If she didn't know better, she would have said that he was behaving as if last Sunday night had never happened.

But it had.

And she had to remember that Jason had always been a brooding loner, she recalled. She suspected that a part of him always would be, even though he'd reached such heights in his career.

She forced herself to turn her attention to the work at hand. The rest was just going to have to work itself out, that's all.

"Robert Abernathy wanted to have a word with you when you were free," she told him. "He called in late last night, after you left."

She stayed late and came in early. That couldn't be good for a woman in her condition. "What were you still doing here?"

"Working," she told him. She looked at him, beginning to feel a little annoyed. What did he think she was doing here? Stealing paper clips?

He started to walk away. There was nothing to be gained by standing here, talking to her. Nothing to be gained and everything to lose. Like his resolve to maintain barriers between them when he wanted nothing more than to break them all down. Nothing more than to take her into his arms and just hold her again.

"Don't overdo it."

That was the second time he'd admonished her. She would have thought that at the very least, after seeing what she could do, he would have wanted her to work at her maximum capacity.

"I wasn't," she told him coolly. "I was just killing time until I had to go to class."

He stopped dead. Immediately he thought of the degree she'd allowed to lie dormant. Was she thinking of pursuing her journalism career and taking some refresher courses to help her on her way? To take her away from here? "You're taking classes?"

She nodded. Why did he sound so surprised? "Over at Manhattan Multiples."

It sounded like the name of a housing complex, not an institution of higher learning. He thought he was up on all of those. "What's that?"

"This wonderful foundation that offers support groups and classes for mothers, parents," she corrected herself, "who are expecting more than one baby. They help prepare you for what's ahead."

He'd noticed that when she said parents, there was a pang in her voice. He tried not to let it get to him. "What's to prepare for? One baby's pretty much like another."

Spoken like a true man, she thought. But then, she couldn't really fault him. He had no children of his own. She'd made a point to ask Nathalie about that, just in case there were more surprises about him.

"Not when they arrive via the group plan they're not," she contradicted. "As soon as I give birth, I'm going to be outnumbered," she told him. And didn't that thought frighten her, she added silently. "That takes some adjustment beyond the usual oh-my-God-what-have-I-done kind of panic they tell me hits most mothers of newborns."

This was the first time she'd said anything about

that. He paused, compassion nudging its way to the top. "Are you panicking?"

There was no point in denying it. "Every day." And then, not wanting to appear like a complete coward, she added, "Just a little. I figure that way I can avoid the final rush at the end of the line." She was gratified to see a small smile play on Jason's lips.

The phone rang just then. Reaching for the receiver, she glanced at Jason. "Looks like your public knows you're in."

It was time to get to work and not stand here, letting his mind wander to places it had no business being. "I'll take it in my office," he told her, signaling an official end to their conversation.

Chapter Thirteen

She'd skipped going to class tonight, hurrying home right after work was over. For once she hadn't stayed late to finish things up.

Timing was everything.

Sitting down on the small sofa that also doubled as her bed, Mindy drew the telephone over to her and placed it on her lap. She took a couple of deep cleansing breaths before she finally began to press the buttons on the telephone keypad, dialing a phone number she was so familiar with.

She was trying to time this so that Brad wasn't home to pick up. It would be a lot easier leaving this as a message on his answering machine than actually talking to him.

It would be a lot easier not calling Brad at all, she thought, but she had to be fair. He needed to know that he was turning his back on twins now, rather than just one child.

God knew she wasn't crediting him with having any paternal feelings at all, she was just following a strict blueprint in her mind. Fathers should be apprised of their children, at least of the number of children they had.

Mentally, she counted off the number of rings. The answering machine was set to four.

At three, she heard a male voice say, ''Hello?''

Her heart dropped like a stone down to her toes. She hadn't gotten the answering machine, she'd gotten Brad.

Shaken, she almost hung up, but the word *coward* echoed fiercely in her head, staying her hand. She wasn't going to run from this.

Looking back, she could see that there were instances when she could have easily been labeled a coward. How many times had she shrunk back from confronting him, from demanding explanations to situations that were highly suspect, even to a woman who wasn't suspicious by nature? Too many to count.

But that had been the old Mindy. The new, improved model took charge of her life, she silently insisted. And that included not turning tail and running from a man she'd once thought herself in love with. A man who obviously had no understanding of what *love* even meant.

She squared her shoulders and straightened her spine. "Brad, it's Mindy."

"Mindy." He sounded surprised and happy to hear from her all at the same time. But the voice that had once delighted her now only produced a feeling of complete apathy within her. "Did your mother tell you I tried to reach you?"

"She mentioned something like that." But she didn't want him to think that was why she was calling. She didn't come when he crooked his finger in her direction, not anymore. "Listen, I—"

He talked right over her. Obviously nothing, she noted cynically, had changed. "Mindy, we need to get together. To talk."

Why? Did your girlfriend suddenly leave? Did you discover you need a date for the weekend?

But she kept her thoughts to herself, determined to keep this civil between them. "Right, we do. And I'm doing it. It's about the baby—"

Again he cut in, sounding nothing short of eager. "You lost it?"

Was that a hopeful note in his voice? Of course it was. Why did she think that it could be anything else? That even if he'd turned out to be a terrible husband, he would somehow make a decent father? This was Brad, and Brad, she'd finally learned, was as self-centered as they came.

What had she ever seen in him?

"No," she replied evenly, working at holding on to her temper, "I didn't lose 'it.'" How like him not to think of the baby as a person, only a thing. He hardly thought of her as a person, either. "I just wanted you to know that there are two babies, Brad." Even now she longed to say "we" but settled for the truth. Other than his initial donation, Brad really wasn't involved in this at all. "I'm having twins."

"Twins?" The echo of disbelief resonated in his voice.

She gave him no chance to accuse her of some kind of elaborate revenge plot. "Yes, and you're no more financially responsible for two of them than you were for one. Goodbye, Brad."

"Mindy, wait—"

But she didn't wait. She disconnected the call before he could say another word.

Replacing the receiver, Mindy smiled to herself. It felt good to hang up on him, the way he had hung up on her emotionally time and time again. Really good.

She'd done the right thing and called him to tell him the newest development, then done the better thing and hung up on him. Now it was really time to get on with the rest of her life.

She felt like a new woman. With an extra ten pounds of frontal baggage, she thought, her hand moving protectively over the area she expected the twins were now huddled. She tried to absorb the feel of her flat abdomen, knowing it was only a matter of time, days probably, until it was no longer flat.

Glancing at her watch, she decided that maybe she

could still catch the tail end of her support group class tonight. It was worth a try.

She couldn't shake the feeling. Try as she might, it just refused to leave, refused to abate.

It had been there now for the better part of a day, and threatened to remain longer.

There was this blue mantle draped over her, almost suffocating her.

Try as she might, Mindy couldn't remember ever feeling so depressed before. It was as if all the bad feelings, all the bad thoughts she'd ever had in her life had converged, forming this massive, oppressive whole that was suffocating her.

She doubted it had anything to do with her call to Brad last night, but that certainly hadn't helped any. Neither had all but getting the cold shoulder from Jason this morning. Just like yesterday morning and the day before that.

Mindy was beginning to think that maybe Jason wasn't so different from her ex after all. Bedding and then moving on seemed to be essentially what he'd done.

Maybe it was the MO of all men; she didn't know. As popular as she'd been in high school and college, her base of sexual experience was severely limited. She had wanted to hold back, to "save herself" for the right man.

The idea seemed ludicrous to her now. Look what

she'd done. She'd saved herself for a womanizer, how pathetic was that?

Almost as pathetic, she thought, as attending classes at Manhattan Multiples alone rather than with someone at her side who cared about her, about her babies. All the other women there seemed to have someone like that with them, why couldn't she?

It didn't seem fair.

She knew it wasn't that uncommon to be a single mother, but all she saw around her whenever she went to Manhattan Multiples were women with partners. If not husbands, then significant others. Everyone had someone. Except for her.

There was no "other" in her life, significant or otherwise. Jason had all but pulled a disappearing act, talking to her these past couple of days as if he'd never touched her, as if all they had in common were the reports she was gathering together for him and the new newsletter he was working on.

As if he'd never made love to her.

Served her right for hoping. Feeling almost volatilely emotional, she dragged her hand through her hair.

God, she didn't want to face walking through those doors alone tonight.

Mindy felt tears gathering in her eyes and she reached for the box of tissues on her desk. The pop-up variety, the next tissue up had somehow lost its ability to stand above the crowd. Even as she tried to pull it out, it hung on tenaciously, surrendering itself to her only in pieces.

She sniffed, battling back the sob that suddenly threatened to break free.

"What's the matter?"

She jumped at the sound of Jason's voice.

His door open, he'd been drawn to the sniffling sound right outside his office completely against his will. But as much as he wanted to pretend he didn't hear it, that it hadn't worked its way under his skin and made a direct hit to his conscience, he couldn't make himself ignore it. Couldn't make himself ignore her. Especially if she sounded as if she was crying.

Freezing, Mindy kept her face forward and down, refusing to let him see her like this. "I can't get the tissue up," she mumbled.

He cocked his head, wondering if he'd just heard her correctly. "That isn't a reason to cry."

When she finally raised her head, she saw that Jason had come around from behind her and was now looking squarely at her. Squarely at the tracks of tears she knew left a freshly marked path down her cheeks.

Angry, upset, she swiped at them with the back of her hand. "I'm sorry, I'm being emotional." She fished up only part of her excuse. "Just my hormones running amok. I didn't mean to disturb you."

"You didn't. You're not."

Actually, that was a lie. She had been disturbing him. Even when she wasn't there, she'd been disturbing him. Disturbing the peace he was trying so vainly to cultivate in his mind. He debated retreating. It was the safest thing to do.

But he couldn't just leave her like this. Especially when he had a feeling that lazy tissues were not the issue here.

So he plunged forward, even as he knew he shouldn't. "Mindy, what's wrong?"

"Wrong?" She tried to sound innocent and failed miserably.

He deliberately fished out another tissue, a whole one this time, and handed it to her. "You're not crying over tissues."

To take it and use it would be a dead giveaway, so she just moved her head away slightly, hoping that evaporation would, for once, work at the speed of lightning and get her out of this jam. "I'm not crying."

The hell she wasn't. Tilting her head back, Jason moved his thumb along her cheek, wiping away a tear that had just stubbornly fallen to contradict her.

"Yes, you are." His eyes searched her face. Was she crying because of him? He needed to know even as guilt riddled through him. "Now, tell me, what's wrong?"

"Wrong?" she repeated incredulously, struggling not to laugh harshly. "What could possibly be wrong? Just because I'm the only single woman at class in a situation that calls for pairs, why should that turn me into competition for the Hoover Dam?"

He was trying to follow her. "Are you talking

about the classes you're attending at that place for multiple births?''

She sniffed. Control was returning, and with it a shred of the dignity that had fled.

''Awkwardly stated, but yes, the classes I'm taking at that place for multiple births. It's called Manhattan Multiples,'' she informed him, ''and I'm called an idiot for getting so emotional. Sorry,'' she said crisply, ''it won't happen again.''

Her tone was clearly dismissive, but he remained where he was, regarding her thoughtfully. Saying something next that he knew he was going to regret. But not saying it would leave her in an uncomfortable place, and he wasn't willing to do that. Like as not, they'd crossed a threshold together and it was difficult to think of her in a detached, distant sort of way, even though he knew it was for the best if he did.

''When do you have to go again?''

She opened a file and tried to concentrate on what was in it. ''Tonight.''

He resisted the temptation to raise her head until she was looking at him. Instead, he kept his arms crossed. ''And you don't want to go alone.''

A careless shoulder rose and fell in response to his question. ''I don't have much choice. Besides, I won't exactly be alone.'' Pausing, Mindy looked down at her stomach. Sight unseen, she already loved the two tenants who dwelled there. ''I have them.''

Always looking for middle ground, he made a tentative stab at a solution. ''Why don't you get your mother to go with you?''

She looked at him as if he'd just suggested she attend the meeting naked.

''Not the same thing.'' In some ways, his solution was worse than the problem. ''Besides, I'm trying to keep her from taking over every facet of my life. She's a wonderful woman and I love her dearly, but you know that cliché about give an inch and they take a mile? Well, right under it in the dictionary there's a photograph of my mother.''

He laughed, any ice that might have still be floating around dissolved. ''What about if someone else went with you?''

That was the whole problem. ''There is no one else to ask.''

He didn't quite see it that way. ''Why don't you ask me?''

''You?'' She stared at him, stunned and certain that she had misheard.

He tried hard not to laugh at the look on her face. ''That's what I just said.''

What was he trying to do, play with her mind? First cool and then hot, then cool and now this? What was she supposed to think? How was she supposed to act? ''I had the impression that you didn't want me to ask you anything. I mean, other than 'Will you take this next call, Mr. Mallory,' of course.''

There was no sense in trying to explain. ''Sorry if

I gave you that impression. I've been under a lot of pressure lately.''

It wasn't a lie, not really. The pressure had been self-made, and a great deal of it did concern her. And some of it involved the guilt he still carried around with him for being ultimately responsible for Debra's death.

But none of that was Mindy's fault, and he didn't want to burden her with it.

She was trying to understand, to absolve him of any blame. Or guilt. ''This business creates a great deal of responsibility.''

He almost contradicted her, almost said that wasn't what he meant, but then he let it go. It was better for both of them if she believed what she'd just said. He paused, waiting. ''Well?''

''Well, what?'' She looked around her desk. Was there something she'd forgotten to do? Some schedule she'd failed to work up?

Did pregnant women usually have the attention span of a pencil, or was she just pulling his leg? ''I'm waiting for you to ask me.''

He couldn't mean what she thought he meant, and if he didn't, then she had no idea what he was driving at. ''Ask you what?''

Maybe pregnant women *did* have the attention span of a pencil, at least when it came to themselves. ''To go to this thing with you.'' It occurred to him that he really had no idea what he was volunteering for. Only for who. ''This class or whatever it is.''

"You'd go with me?" Even as she said it, she still couldn't believe it.

"Well, not if you don't ask. I wouldn't know where to go."

Despite her best intentions, her mouth dropped open. "Straight to the head of the class," she murmured. *Yes, Virginia, there really is a Santa Claus. And he wears special tailored suits and has warm, brown eyes and a dimple in his cheek when he smiles. And you can't have him because he's mine. I think.* She looked at him uncertainly. "You're not joking?"

He allowed himself the smallest of smiles as he looked at her disbelieving expression. "Mindy, how many times have you known me to joke?"

"Not nearly often enough," was her honest response. "Then you're actually willing to go? To attend this birthing class with me?"

"Yes." And then, because he'd been practical all of his life, he added a codicil. "As long as I don't have to do anything strange."

Cocking her head just slightly, she kept her eyes on his. "Define *strange*."

He could think of one thing right off the top of his head. He definitely didn't want to be grossed out, especially not in the company of strangers. "Is there going to be a video?"

His question made her grin. It had been one of her concerns, as well, when she'd signed up for the class. "That doesn't happen for a couple of months. I think they're waiting for us to be too huge to get out of our chairs and run for the exits before they show it.'' She could feel herself growing excited now. And hopeful. ''You won't even have to talk,'' she promised him. ''Just be there.''

''What good is that?''

''The greatest good in the world,'' she assured him. ''You'll be providing me with moral support.'' Not to mention that his presence would erase that awful, empty feeling she'd been battling every time she walked into the classroom alone.

She was the last person in the world he would have guessed needed moral support. The woman was forged out of confidence. ''What time do you want me to pick you up?''

She wanted to make this as simple as possible for him. To encourage him not to make this a one-shot deal. ''I usually go straight from here.''

''Well, I guess it can't get any easier than that.'' He had some things planned for this evening and wondered if he'd get a chance to squeeze them in. ''What time is the class?''

''Seven.'' She'd noted him looking at his watch. She knew all his appointments, had handled them all herself, so if he was trying to carve out some time for himself, it involved something personal. Like a woman. She searched his face. ''Is that all right?''

''That'll be fine. We can stop for a light dinner first if you'd like,'' he suggested. ''Or after it's over if you're not supposed to attend these classes on a full stomach.''

"I already have a full stomach," she reminded him, rubbing the palm of her hand over her abdomen now. "Before would be nice."

"Before it is." The phone rang, bringing him mentally back to the office. Not quite tearing him away from her. "That would be my two-o'clock conference call with World Net Savings's CEO."

She reached for the receiver, nodding. It amazed her how on top of things this man was. He was aware of every appointment, every meeting, never forgetting anything. "I'll put it through."

It also occurred to her, as she picked up the receiver, that had things gone differently for both of them all those years ago, Jason could have been attending these meetings with her in earnest.

She tucked the thought away. Again.

Jason looked as if he fit right in, she thought. Sitting beside her on a folding chair, wearing his light-gray designer suit, not even loosening his blue silk tie, he still looked as if he fit right in. As if he could have been one of these nervous, expectant fathers who were sitting silently, or not so silently, beside their wives, trying to absorb the magnitude of what was about to happen to them in their lives.

With all her heart she found herself wishing that these were his babies she was carrying. She instinctively knew that Jason would make a wonderful father when the time came. There was just something about him. It wouldn't be anything that he'd advertise, just something that he'd be.

Just like he was sitting here with her when he didn't have to be. She would never have asked him if he hadn't all but put the words into her mouth.

He was better than she expected him to be. And she was falling in love with him, she thought.

What, falling? She'd already reached her destination and had moved in, utterly uninvited. She knew that she was setting herself up for a fall, but right at this moment, with him beside her, she didn't care.

She figured that would come later.

Chapter Fourteen

The scent of Mindy's perfume, soft and seductive, filled the interior of his car. Caused the core of his gut to tighten so that drawing a full breath was a test of both will and strength.

He was taking her home now and as far as evenings went, this had been an education for him. He'd learned a few things, both about having twins and about himself. He wanted children. It was an odd thing to discover this about yourself at the age of twenty-nine. He would have thought that he knew himself as well as could possibly be expected, but he didn't. Having a family had never really entered into his plans before. Debra hadn't wanted children, and that had been fine with him.

It wasn't fine anymore.

The fragrance teased his senses, heightening his awareness that there was only so much space within the car. That he had only to reach out his right hand to touch her.

It was hard not to.

He'd missed her, he thought. Missed Mindy even though he'd seen her each day at work. Missed just sitting quietly with her, watching the light caress her skin, watching expressions come and go over her animated, intriguing face.

Missed her.

He brought the car to a stop at a light and glanced in Mindy's direction. Wanting things he shouldn't. Wanting a life he had no claim to.

When their eyes met, Jason felt he had to say something. He thought of her class. "You're going to need help."

The comment, coming out of nowhere after several minutes of silence as they wove their way through the clog that passed as evening traffic, took her by surprise. "At work?"

She thought they'd already had this discussion more than two weeks ago. By all indications she felt she was holding up her end at the office rather well. Nathalie had certainly found no fault in her. Jason's flamboyant partner had made a point of stopping by her desk and praising her several times.

"No," he told her, "at home." He felt his patience ebbing as cars dribbled through the intersection, moving as slowly as the humid air right outside his air-conditioned vehicle.

She thought of the size of her apartment. It took her exactly an hour to clean it from top to bottom. What she needed help in, if anything, was to keep from feeling claustrophobic, not that she would ever admit that to her mother.

Her eyebrows drew together as she looked at his profile. "What do you mean?"

"With the twins. When they arrive, I mean. Obviously."

Damn it, he was tripping over his own tongue again. Frustration nibbled away at him. There was something about being with her that stripped him of any artificial eloquence he might have acquired during his business years, turning him back into that guy who was forced to watch her from a distance. Yearning.

He tried again. "After that session tonight…it doesn't sound as if you're going to get any sleep for the next four years."

Jason glanced at her a second before he eased his foot off the brake and back onto the gas. His thigh was beginning to ache from the continuous transfer. They probably could have made better time if they'd walked. Given the impact of the weather, however, they would have undoubtedly arrived at their destination pounds lighter.

His laugh was self-deprecating. "I'm not making things any easier for you, bringing that up, am I?"

His awkward verbal stumbling, after she'd seen him conduct himself with aplomb, fielding questions that flew at him hard and fast from savvy CEOs struck her as endearing.

"You're not saying anything that hasn't already crossed my mind several times over," she assured him. "But it'll be all right. Manhattan Multiples offers a wonderful day-care service, so when I'm ready to go back to work, I don't have to worry about who is going to watch my babies." She wanted him to know that she hadn't changed her mind about returning. How could she? She needed the money and she needed to see him, not necessarily in that order. "And I've got a cousin in the city who's a stay-at-home mom. She's already offered to be there for me whenever I need to grab a little personal time or make a stab at reestablishing my sanity." She smiled at him. "I'll be okay."

It was almost as if she was trying to comfort him, he realized. "That's supposed to be my job. Trying to make you feel better, not the other way around." They moved another foot closer to her building.

Mindy didn't bother trying to stifle the laugh. "You can take the next shift," she promised. Moving in her seat, she adjusted the seat belt slightly. Was she getting larger even as they were driving? "Actually, you have made me feel better, just by coming with me." He probably thought she was getting flaky on him. "I'm sorry, I didn't mean to breakdown like that in the office today."

He was actually glad that she had. It had given him an excuse to see her tonight. An excuse he could live with. "That wasn't a breakdown, that was hardly a pause, really. And someone in your situation is entitled to vent their emotions once in a while." He slanted a look at her. "You're shouldering a lot."

He was being kind about it, and she appreciated it more than words could express. "All the same, thanks for being understanding." She blew out a breath, thinking of Brad. "A lot of men wouldn't be."

He could tell by her tone exactly what was on her mind. "A lot of men would be stupid, then." Maybe it was the night encroaching on him, or maybe it was just that he had spent so long pushing the memory away that it had suddenly boomeranged and came back at him. Whatever the reason, guilt came flooding over him. "But don't make me out to be a saint, Mindy. I'm far from that."

"Skin cats in your spare time, do you?" She watched his profile, expecting her teasing comment to produce a smile and knock the edge off his voice. But his jaw remained rigid. Concern began to tiptoe in quietly.

"No, a lot worse than that."

He sounded like someone who was tormented. "I'm listening," she told him quietly.

He didn't want to tell her, didn't want her to think badly of him. Why hadn't he just kept his mouth shut? "But I've stopped talking."

She placed a gentle, comforting hand on his leg,

wanting him to know that she was there for him as much as he'd just been there for her.

"Maybe you should start again." When he said nothing, she pushed. She couldn't just retreat, not after hearing the pain in his voice. She wanted to help any way she could. "It *always* helps to get things out into the light of day. It's the dark that makes things unbearable."

He sighed. "I killed my wife." Slanting a glance at her, he saw Mindy's jaw slacken.

There had to be some logical explanation, she thought. Her voice was a tight whisper as she asked, "What are you talking about?"

He wondered if she pictured something dramatic, like him standing over his wife with a gun.

"Oh, not literally. I didn't put my hands around her neck and choke her or anything like that—not that I didn't want to," he admitted. He might as well tell her everything, let her see him with all his warts. He half expected to see her shrink away from him, but she was still sitting there, still waiting, a compassionate expression on her face. How the hell could her husband have walked away from her? "You see, Debra and your husband—"

"Ex-husband," she emphasized.

She and Jason had made love, and she didn't want him thinking that she would have done that if she'd regarded herself as still married to Brad in any sense of the word. Even the ring was gone from her finger. For some reason, just as she was about to go to a jeweler to have her wedding ring cut off, her finger had become accommodating and gone back to its normal size. The ring had come off immediately.

"Ex-husband," he allowed, "had a lot in common. They both had a need to seek their pleasure outside the confines of home." Bitterness sprang up in his chest, spilling out into his words. "In Debra's case, that was the only place she sought any pleasure." He refrained from elaborating and saying that she'd been cold as ice almost from the first. There was no need for Mindy to know that. It was enough to say "That was the reason I was divorcing her."

He hadn't mentioned this before. "You were in the process of divorce when she died?"

That wasn't strictly true. "I was in the process of telling her about it. I called her on her cell phone, saying we had to talk about this sham we called a marriage." He stared into the artificially lit darkness as he continued to herd his car through the traffic. "Those were my last words to her. She was crossing the street, yelling at me about having the audacity to say I was leaving her." His shoulder rose in a half-hearted, careless shrug. "She wasn't paying attention to where she was going. That was when the car hit her." He took a deep breath. "The paramedics who arrived at the scene said she'd died instantly."

It took her a moment to recover. "Oh, Jason, I'm so sorry." But even as she said it, she knew that there was something more important than that to talk about. He held himself responsible for the woman's death.

She could hear it in his voice. ''But it wasn't your fault.''

How could it not be, he wanted to demand. ''If she wasn't talking to me—''

Mindy didn't let him finish. It was time he forgave himself. ''And if I wasn't five foot four doesn't mean that I'd be a six foot blonde. Things happen and we can't predict them,'' she insisted. ''Most of the time we can't even stop them.'' She wasn't getting through. ''If you want to take your argument a step further, if Debra hadn't been stepping out on you, there would have been no need for you to call her and she wouldn't have been on the phone with you when she was crossing the street.'' She wanted to shake him, to make him see how wrong he was. Her voice rose. ''If anything, she's the one who brought it on herself, not you.''

She sounded so sincere, so convinced. He allowed himself to see it through her eyes, if only for a moment. ''When you put it like that—''

''*That* is the only way to put it,'' she insisted. ''Sometimes things just happen for a reason that we don't understand.'' They were approaching her building. Mindy automatically scanned the block, then smiled in triumph. ''Like finding an open spot right in front of my building when the streets are full of people driving around, looking for somewhere to park.''

Because for the moment the tension had left his

body, because it was so nice just being here with her, he laughed. "Think it's an omen?"

Mindy nodded, her expression suddenly serious. "That would be my guess."

For a brief moment he toyed with the idea of coming up. With the idea of letting himself go and making love with her. "I guess if I didn't take advantage of it, I'd be angering the omen gods."

Despite her best efforts, a smile began to creep along her lips. "Right again."

But his world was based on a foundation of control, and he was allowing that to break down. "About the word *advantage*—"

She knew where he was going with this. Amazing how much she had learned about the man in such a short time, she thought. But that only meant that she was destined to be with Jason, because she could intuit what he was going to say.

"To avail oneself of opportunities. I know the definition, Jason. I also know that if it was coupled with the word *unfair* you wouldn't have anything to do with it. It's against your nature."

She didn't know anything about his nature, he thought. He'd always kept himself under wraps too well. "I wouldn't be that sure if I were you."

She wasn't going to let him do this to himself. He was good and kind and she knew this because she'd known the opposite in her time.

"Oh, but I am. Very, very sure." She pointed toward the spot. They were almost on top of it, but she took nothing for granted. Not in this city. "Now hurry up and park there before someone else beats you to it."

He laughed as he lined up his car. "You're beginning to sound like a regular New Yorker."

Her grin was broad and went straight to his heart. "Born and bred." She pretended to level a look at him. "So don't argue with me."

The fit was tight, but he made it with an inch to spare. Finished, he winked at her. "Wouldn't think of it."

She could have sworn she felt the babies move, but knew it was only her reaction to him.

There was no question in Jason's mind that when he brought her to her door, she would be opening it. And that he would be stepping inside.

He'd gone with Mindy to her class to lend a little moral support, but in a surprising reversal of roles, she had been the one to offer it to him instead.

He'd told her things he'd never completely shared with anyone. He felt strangely relieved and vulnerable at the same time. He was fairly confident that come morning, he would shore up his beaches again. But this wasn't morning, this was night and she was particularly enticing to him.

Hell, she'd *always* been enticing to him.

For that reason, because he couldn't trust his own judgment, Jason felt compelled to offer her one last chance to send him away.

Even as he kissed her with every ounce of longing that existed in his soul.

Or maybe because of it.

It took a great deal of effort to separate himself from her. "I should go," he murmured.

The words, encased in his warm breath, slid seductively against her lips. Stimulating her.

She moved her head from side to side as she entwined her arms around his neck and brought him back to her. "You should stay."

God knew he wanted to. He made no move to go, smiling instead into her eyes. Savoring the feel of her against his body. "Does anyone ever win an argument with you?"

"Not when it counts."

She didn't want him to think that she was trying to pressure him. Or that all she had thought about for the whole of the evening, throughout dinner, the class and then the ride home, had been making love with him. Stepping back, she looked around her small living quarters. The leftovers her mother had insisted on making her take home were still in the refrigerator.

"Can I offer you something?" When he didn't answer immediately, she looked at him and saw the smile. And read his mind because it was in sync with hers. "That goes without saying."

Right at this moment she felt very, very close to him. He'd shared something with her that she had a feeling he didn't ordinarily tell anyone. That brought them to a very intimate place. Whether that was only temporary or signaled the beginning of a new level for them, she could only guess, could only hope. But all she knew was that tonight, she was there. *They* were there and she wanted to make the most of it.

Food was the last thing on his mind. As she moved toward the refrigerator, Jason took her into his arms. He wanted her so badly that he was having difficulty breathing.

He looked around the snug room. ''Where are you going to put the cribs?''

It took effort to keep her mind on the question when her body was melting against his. ''Well, at first, since they're going to be little, there'll only be one crib. And I guess it'll go next to the sofa.'' She frowned, looking down at the only other flat surface in the room besides her small table. ''That means the coffee table is going to have to go.''

Even so, that didn't give her enough room, he thought. His fingers slowly slid along her cheek. ''You need a bigger apartment you know.''

Damn but he could decompose the consistency of her knees faster than anyone she'd ever met. She leaned into him. Absorbing his warmth, allowing desires to shoot through her.

''That's something I'll face later. I'm already checking the obituaries.''

''I've got three bedrooms and a lot of space I don't know what to do with.''

She knew he had an apartment in SoHo. Nathalie

had mentioned it to her in passing. Only half in jest, she asked, "Are you proposing a trade?"

Jason plunged in, knowing that if he thought it through, he might not make the offer.

"Not exactly. I'm proposing you move in with me." He saw her eyes widen. Was that surprise, or was she desperately trying to find a way to gracefully decline his offer? He hurried to state his case. "I mean, it's only logical. You don't have enough space to turn around in, I have enough space to house the traveling company of The Fantastiks." And then it occurred to him that she might misunderstand the nature of his offer. He was making it strictly from a practical standpoint. He wanted her to be comfortable. "It can be purely platonic if you like."

Was she sending the wrong signals to him? "What makes you think that I'd like it to be platonic?"

Unable to hold himself in check any longer, he brushed a kiss against her throat. "I don't want you to think I'm trading space for sex."

Mindy dug her fingers into his shoulders, trying to anchor her mind for a little longer before it became a free-floating entity in space.

"I never realized in high school that you had such a droll sense of humor." He was playing havoc with her senses. To counteract the assault, she kissed him. "It's a very generous offer—"

"But?" He could hear the hesitation in her voice.

She framed his face with her hands, her heart swelling. If this wasn't love she was feeling, then she didn't know what was.

"But I think you made it on the spur of the moment." He began to protest, and she placed her finger against his lips. "I'm going to let you think about this before I say yes." And she really wanted to say yes, but she'd been quick to do that before, with Brad. Maybe they both needed a little time to let things settle. "Sleep on it tonight if you will."

He began to toy with the zipper at the back of her dress. "I wasn't thinking about sleeping just now."

The smile on her lips feathered into her eyes as it deepened. "Good, because neither was I." Her pulse was already racing.

Things were going very, very fast. Above all, he didn't want to take advantage of her. Didn't want her to feel that he was. "If you want me to stop—"

Her eyes sparkled. "You really aren't any good at mind reading, are you?" Her hands on either side of his face, she kissed him hard and with all the emotion that was bubbling up within her, threatening to spill out and drench them both.

She made his head spin. Made his heart swell with dreams and a desire for a more innocent time, when he could have just offered her the world and himself without any excess baggage attached.

Drawing his head back to look at her, he smiled. "I am now."

With that, he brought his mouth down to hers

again. Holding her to him with one hand, he resumed undoing the zipper of her summery dress. As it slid down to the base of her spine, he could feel excitement seizing him, traveling up and down the length of his body like a bolt of lightning searching for somewhere to explode.

The very scent of her heated his blood. He had to caution himself to hold back, to take it slow when all he wanted to do was race to the end, to when he could possess her, body and soul.

But that would be selfish of him, and the last thing he wanted to do was be selfish with her.

The very taste of her mouth felt as if it enriched the texture of his life and he wanted to give her back a little in kind. Wanted to erase any of the doubts she might still possess about herself as a result of the way that worthless jerk had treated her.

But if it hadn't been for that worthless jerk, he realized, she wouldn't be here with him now. So, in a way, he had to be grateful that her ex had turned out to be such a loser. He only wished Mindy hadn't suffered because of it.

That was his responsibility, Jason realized, to take away any of the pain she might have endured because of her ex.

And, in so doing, in making love with her, he managed to also erase so much of the pain, so much of the damage that having been in love with Debra had produced for him. Because in making love with

Mindy, everything else paled in comparison. Paled so that it completely disappeared from his brain.

He lost himself in her. In the sound of her breath entering and leaving her lungs, in the curves of her body that were just beginning to swell with the promise of life. In the dusky tastes that rose up to greet him as he kissed every inch of her.

Somehow they'd wound up naked and on the floor rather than the sofa. It seemed impossibly decadent to her. As did the feelings racing through her. She'd been completely inexperienced when she'd come to her husband's bed, and he hadn't exactly been a patient teacher. Yet now, because of Jason, there were thoughts, desires entering her brain, coming from nowhere, that took her completely by surprise. Instincts rather than knowledge or experience guided her hand, her body, schooling her in erotic movements that were reducing both of them to pulsating masses of heat and desire.

Trying desperately to draw enough air into her lungs to continue, Mindy straddled him, her body moving along his in an impossibly erotic invitation. Enflaming him. Doing the same to her.

He'd already brought her to the pinnacle twice, and she knew he was holding himself back. She wanted to entice him, to make him ache for her. With slow, deliberate movements, she swayed over him. Feeling him harden even more.

Jason reached up for her. ''Where did you learn all this?'' he murmured.

Her eyes were shining as she took him into her. ''From you.''

He cried out her name against her ear as she drove him over the brink. And took her with him to the private land they both needed to inhabit.

Chapter Fifteen

She was going to give notice. Logically, there was nothing else she could do.

Except that logic had very little to do with it. The root of the problem was all wrapped up in her emotions. She felt like an emotional Ping-Pong ball, continually being lobbed back and forth over an imaginary net. And now the ball had sailed completely out of her court and disappeared.

It had been three days since Jason had been to her apartment, three days since he'd made love with her. Three days since he'd offered to have her move into his apartment. And not only hadn't he mentioned it, he hadn't even been to the office in all that time.

It was as if he'd suddenly gone into hiding, afraid

that she would take him up on his offer, an offer she now knew he'd made on the spur of the moment, without thinking it through. She'd known it then, but that hadn't stopped her from hoping.

That was the problem.

Hope.

It was the cruelest of all emotions. It buoyed you up, made you believe that something better was possible and then suddenly let you fall from heights you would have never risen to if it hadn't been for hope to begin with.

Well, she was through with all that, through with thinking that things were going to get better for her because she'd given away her heart to someone. The only person she could truly rely on was herself, and she couldn't do that if she kept slipping up like this. If she kept hoping against hope.

Which meant, Mindy decided, that she was going to have to quit her job even though it had been hard to come by. Even though she was good at it and loved it. She couldn't continue working here and survive. If quitting meant accepting her parents' help for a little while, well, that couldn't be helped. At least with her parents, she knew where she stood. They weren't going to trample her newly displayed heart as if it was some kind of a runway to be stomped on. All they cared about was that she was happy and secure.

That obviously wasn't a concern for Jason. All he cared about was ducking for cover.

He'd have plenty of that once she was gone, she

thought. No more emotional hide-and-seek games. No more making her feel as if she could fly only to yank away the parachute and let her free fall to earth.

Mindy Conway, she declared silently as she marched into Nathalie's office, was not about to go splat for anyone.

Not even for the man she loved.

Exhausted, Jason struggled to keep his eyes open as the taxi he'd picked up at JFK went into the last leg of its trip. One of the downsides of his business was the need to suddenly fly off at a moment's notice. After he'd gotten home from Mindy's Monday night, he'd found a message on his answering machine that had him calling the airport to book an immediate flight to California. He'd gone to check out firsthand whether or not the rumors of an eminent CEO's underhanded deals were true. A positive answer would have signaled yet another tumble of a major corporate empire. If that was about to happen, his clients relied on him to apprise them of the situation as soon as humanly possible.

But after all his exhaustive digging and touching upon all the sources he'd carefully cultivated over the years, he had unearthed a different truth. An ugly one. For reasons of his own profit, someone within the company was attempting to discredit the CEO by planting the rumors. The intent was that in these trying times, the hint of wrongdoing was enough to get a man thrown from grace. The rumormonger was trying to capitalize on the created situation by trading down on the sly.

Jason had exposed the plot, reporting the whole thing to the people who mattered at the SEC.

He felt a little like a detective. Jason had stayed exactly long enough to file the report and accept one thank-you, then he'd hopped on a plane bound for JFK. The job had all but consumed him for the past three days, so much so that all he'd had time for was to call Nathalie and leave a message on her answering machine. He'd called Mindy, too, but had gotten neither her machine nor her.

Which was just as well. He decided that he would hold off calling her. What he wanted to say to her was best said in person. On the flight to L.A., he'd changed his mind about having her move in with him. He didn't want her to simply move in, he wanted her to marry him. That wasn't the kind of question you asked over the telephone or via e-mail. That was the kind of thing that you stuttered through in person.

And he had no doubt that he would stutter. Baring his soul had never been an easy thing for him to do, but hell, it was something he knew was well worth it. All his previous hesitation had vanished, along with the guilt he'd shouldered for so long. Mindy had seen to that. He knew now that Mindy wasn't Debra. She was by far the best thing that ever happened to him, and the moment he got into the office, he was going to whisk her aside to tell her that. Along with proposing to her.

That was why he was coming in straight from the airport, without even stopping by his apartment to shower or change his clothes. He was rumpled, tired and wired, but he was also the happiest he'd ever been.

Until the moment he walked into the office and saw the empty desk.

His carry-on luggage slipped from his fingers, unnoticed. Mindy's chair was pushed up against the desk. There was nothing but an uncluttered blotter and a computer gracing the space. No indication that Mindy was in for the day. Or even that she'd ever been there. All the small touches that she had brought in, the vertically challenged stuffed dog that looked down at her monitor as she typed, the framed photograph of her sonogram of the twins, all that was gone. It could have been anyone's desk.

Or no one's.

He had a bad feeling about this.

"Nathalie." He called out his partner's name as he strode toward her office. Not standing on formality, he yanked open her door and walked in.

Nathalie was in a meeting with one of the interns. The moment she saw Jason's face, she braced herself, as if she knew what was coming.

Her eyes never leaving Jason's face, Nathalie told the intern she'd talk to him later. The latter had enough sense to leave immediately, quickly ducking by Jason as he went.

Jason hardly noticed the younger man. "Where is she?" he demanded.

Nathalie knew better than to ask who, or to even attempt to calm him down. She faced him the way she would face down an angry investor. "Gone."

"Gone? What do you mean gone?" The single word had no meaning for him. Even as he repeated it, it refused to penetrate his brain. "Gone where? You mean gone for the day?"

Nathalie shook her head. "Gone permanently. She came in and gave me her notice last night. Said she wouldn't be in this morning. That she was taking the one day she'd earned as a vacation day and that she wasn't coming back."

Why? Why would Mindy suddenly just leave? When he'd left, everything looked as if it was finally in the right place. Now it was all falling apart. He focused on Nathalie. "What did you do to her?"

Nathalie's hands went up as if to ward off any blame. "Hey, I've done nothing but encourage her since she came in for the interview." Her eyes pinned him. "I'm not the one who kept changing sides."

Jason resisted the urge to pace around the room. He felt confused, restless. Scared. "What are you talking about?"

Rounding her desk, Nathalie placed her hands on Jason's back and pushed him toward the door. "Don't play dumb with me, Jason. There isn't time for that. Go talk to her if you want her to change her mind. Maybe she'll listen to you. She sure wasn't listening to me when I tried to talk her into staying. I told her we couldn't do without her. She said you were doing very well on your own." Her look was accusing. "My take on it is that you left her dangling in the wind. Again."

He had no idea how much Nathalie actually knew about what had gone on between him and Mindy. Probably more than he was comfortable with. But there was no time to ask questions. "No dangling," he insisted. "I was away on business."

"Does Mindy know that?"

"I didn't tell her, if that's what you mean."

She looked at him, a lawyer who'd won her case. "Well then?"

In the doorway, looking toward the elevator, Jason hesitated. He was torn between what he wanted to do and what he had to do. "I've got to get an e-mail out to our subscribers."

Nathalie gave him another push, sending him over the threshold. "Dictate it to me on your way to the elevator," she instructed. "In case you haven't noticed, I've got ten fingers." She held them up in front of his face to illustrate her point. "All of them built for typing."

Punching the button for the elevator, he gave her the upshot of the investigation, minimizing his own part in it. The car arrived almost immediately.

"Just make it short and sweet." Getting in, he held the door open with one hand. "End it by saying I'll send more later."

Nathalie waved him back so that the doors could close. ''Fine, fine, we'll survive this crisis. We've survived all the others. Now let the elevator go,'' she peeled back his fingers, ''and go tell Mindy you love her.''

He looked at her in surprise as the doors started to shut. ''I never said that.''

''You didn't have to,'' she countered quickly just before the doors closed.

Mindy's heart dropped down to the bottom of her shoes. When she'd heard the knock on the door, she'd hurried to throw it open. Despite all her warnings to herself, she was hoping against hope that it was Jason, come to sweep her up in his arms. To tell her he couldn't live without her. Twenty-eight years old and she was still living in a fantasy world, she upbraided herself.

Her own words rose up to mock her now as she looked at the man at her door.

Not Jason.

The words echoed in her head as she resisted the urge to let the door slam in his face. ''Brad, what are you doing here?''

Not waiting for an invitation, Brad strode in. The slight, triumphant smirk he wore on his face as he looked around the room was not lost on her. But when he turned to face her, his expression had become the soul of contrition.

He'd always been a good actor, she thought. Certainly good enough to fool her. But not anymore.

He reached for her hand, but she pulled it away before he could take it. ''I've come to ask you to give our marriage another chance.''

It wasn't what she'd expected him to say.

Mindy stared at him for a long moment. Beyond shock, there was nothing. She felt nothing. She didn't feel sentimental, she didn't even feel angry. Nothing. Since she'd packed up and left her house, she'd worked everything out, felt everything she was going to feel for and about Brad, and now she was devoid of any and all feelings. Other than wanting him to leave.

''I did, Brad.'' She remained at the door, waiting for him to use it. ''I gave it another chance. I gave it lots of chances. But you can't have your wife and your bachelorhood, too.'' And it was clearly the latter that he wanted.

''That's what I've come here to tell you.'' Sincerity all but dripped from his voice. ''I just want you, not all the others.''

Mindy regarded him coolly, wondering what she'd ever seen in him. Wondering why she'd sacrificed her own career just to help support his. The man was so transparent. This wasn't about missing her or doing the right thing. This was still just about him.

''Why, Brad? Because Mr. Willis told you to straighten up your act?'' She knew that Brad's regional manager was a stickler for family values. Something that Brad was obviously lacking.

Brad's mouth dropped open. ''How did you know? I mean—''

When she thought of all the years she'd wasted... But there was no point in regretting the past. Only in building a future.

''You're a very smooth operator, Brad.'' She saw the wary look enter his eyes. ''No, I mean that, really. And I think you did miss your calling. You should be selling used cars instead of insurance.'' And then the smile faded from her lips. ''But I don't want a used car anymore, Brad. Or a used husband.''

It was evident that he wasn't going to give up so easily. ''I'll change.''

She laughed shortly. Right, and she was going to fly any second now. ''Not that I think you could, but there's no reason to change. I've outgrown you, Brad. I don't want to be your little Stepford wife any more. I want to be me, a full person, not half of one.''

Impatience creased his handsome features. ''Look, we can iron all that out later, just come back with me now.''

Mindy remained steadfast. The hardest thing she'd ever done was leave Brad. But now that she had, she knew it had been the right thing to do. ''Nope, there's not going to be a later.''

Brad made a last-ditch attempt to show her that she really cared. ''You still have my wedding ring—''

She was infinitely grateful that she'd managed to

get the ring off when she did. ''Don't try to make anything out of that. It was merely an oversight.'' She nodded toward the door in the far corner. ''I've got it stashed in the bathroom.'' She saw his puzzled expression. ''Every day I get up and think about flushing it down the toilet.''

Horror replaced confusion. Mindy knew the ring had set him back an ungodly amount. But it had nothing to do with her, she knew, and everything to do with the facade he was attempting to display to the world.

''But you won't.'' He seemed to be holding his breath.

''No, I won't,'' Mindy agreed. ''But only because it would clog the pipes if I did.'' He started to follow her to the bathroom. ''Wait right here,'' she instructed. ''And I'll get it.''

All the way over from the office, Jason rehearsed what he wanted to say to Mindy. He'd flagged down a taxi the moment he'd hit the street, even though the company car was in the parking structure and available to him. He didn't want to waste time looking for a place to park once he reached her building.

All he wanted to do was sweep her into his arms. And he would, the moment he saw her.

Jason refused to contemplate the possibility that she might not be there. The very idea left him cold.

But in all the scenarios he did go over in his mind

as the taxi crawled to its destination, never once did another man enter into it.

Another man like the one who opened the door to Mindy's apartment when he rang the bell.

Something froze within Jason. The unearthly sensation of déjà vu came over him, but he shook it off. "I'm sorry," he heard himself say, "I must have the wrong apartment."

The good-looking man stared at him, his hand on the door, barring any farther access into the apartment. "Who are you looking for?"

Was she inside? Was she standing behind the door so he couldn't see her? Was this the reason she'd quit? "Mindy Conway."

The man's eyes narrowed. "You mean Mindy Richards," he corrected. And then he delivered the fatal blow. "She's my wife."

Jason could feel the air suddenly becoming solid in his throat, threatening to choke him. She'd told him the divorce papers had gone through. Was that a lie? "Your wife? You're Brad?"

"Yes, why?" Brad regarded him belligerently. "What do you want with her?"

He wasn't going to get in the middle of this, Jason thought. It was obvious that Mindy had made her choice and he wasn't going to ruin it for her.

Not matter what it cost him.

"Nothing," he said stiffly. "She just worked for me, that's all." Because the statement begged for a follow-up, he added, "I've been away and when I came back, I found out Mindy had given notice. I thought that maybe I could change her mind, but that's clearly not the case.'' He backed away from the door. ''Just tell her to have a nice life.''

With that, Jason turned away and headed for the elevator. He punched the button.

Her husband. She was getting back with her husband. They'd made love on Monday night, and there was someone else in the wings all along.

Just like with Debra.

Damn it, how could he have been such a fool? Twice.

The elevator opened and he stormed in.

''Here.''

Walking out of the bathroom, Mindy thrust her wedding ring at her ex as if it was a piece of cheap costume jewelry instead of something that had set him back almost five thousand dollars. She'd hidden the ring in the back of the cabinet beneath the sink for safekeeping, and it had taken some rearranging to get at it.

''Now you can go.'' She noticed that her door was ajar. While reaching under the cabinet, she'd thought she'd heard the doorbell ring. Mindy looked at Brad. ''Was there someone at the door?''

Brad shrugged carelessly, his attention focused on the ring in his hand. He looked as if he was examining it to see if all the stones were in place. ''Some guy. Said you worked for him.''

Mindy's eyes widened. Jason? Jason was here? Then he *had* come. And talked to Brad. Her heart sank. She grabbed Brad's arm to get his attention. "What else did he say?"

"To have a nice life."

Oh God, Mindy thought. That's what he'd written to her in her yearbook. And then they hadn't seen each other for eleven years. She had to get to him, had to stop him before it was too late.

Brad hurried after her. "He said you quit, that means you were coming back to me."

"Never," Mindy shouted over her shoulder, running into the hall.

But he was gone.

Mindy hurried to the elevator. The indicator showed that it was going down.

Brad was still breathing down her neck. "Go home, Brad," she yelled as she threw open the door to the stairwell. "Now!"

Holding on to the banister, Mindy ran down the two flights of stairs as fast as she could, but when she arrived at the first floor, the elevator had gotten there ahead of her. It stood open, its lone passenger having just disembarked.

Her heart was pounding hard as Mindy raced out onto the street. Frantically, she looked in both directions and almost cried when she spotted him. Jason was walking toward 72nd Street.

"Jason!" she yelled. But if he heard her, he gave

no indication. The noise of the city swallowed up her voice. "Jason!"

When he still didn't turn around, she began to run after him, hoping she wouldn't break a heel. Why hadn't she worn sneakers this morning?

Sprinting, Mindy managed to catch up to him just before he crossed the street. Grabbing his arm, she yanked Jason around.

She was panting as she said, "Don't you know you shouldn't make a pregnant woman run?"

Her cheeks were flushed and her hair was plastered against her face. She looked as if she'd just dashed through a sprinkler system. He wanted to take her into his arms but held back. She didn't belong to him.

"What are you doing out here?" he asked.

"Chasing you."

Jason jerked a thumb toward the building in the middle of the block. "Your husband's upstairs, why aren't you with him?"

Still dragging air back into her lungs, she could only stare at Jason. "With him? Why would you send me back to him?"

Why was she doing this to him? He didn't need to be jerked around like this. "He's the father of your children."

There was no question about that. Nor about the rest of it. "He's also a self-centered womanizer. We decided that at the convention, remember?" Didn't Jason care about her at all? But then, if he didn't, why had he come over? ''Is that the kind of man you want to send me back to?''

''I thought you and he were back together.'' Anger creased his brow.

He wasn't making any sense. ''Why would you think that?''

Now he really was angry. ''Mindy, the man lives in Illinois. It's not like he was just in the neighborhood and decided to drop by.''

What did that have to do with anything? ''I can't be responsible for what he does or where he goes, Jason.'' The protest struck her as ironic. ''Any more than I could when we were married.'' He was trying to change the subject; she wasn't going to let him. ''But his location isn't the issue here.'' Mindy took the offensive, jabbing a finger at him. ''Why would you just leave me with him?''

''Because I thought that was what you wanted and I want you to be happy.'' He grabbed her finger as she went to poke him again. The next words tumbled out before he could stop them. ''I love you.''

''If you loved me, you'd fight for me, damn it, not throw me to the wolf.'' And then the magnitude of what she'd just glossed over hit her. Her eyes widened. ''Hold it, did you just say you loved me?''

''Yes.''

But he'd just gone three days without surfacing once. ''When did this happen?''

That was easy enough to answer. His voice softened. ''The first day I ever saw you.''

All the anger, all the hurt, melted instantly. The oppressive heat had nothing to do with it. She smiled at him. ''Not exactly fast, are you?''

''What I lack in speed, I make up in tenacity.'' He'd overreacted, he thought. Relief was swift in coming. ''So, you're not getting together?''

''No.''

He needed to get things straight. ''But you are quitting.''

She shrugged helplessly. The man needed to come with an instruction manual. ''I figured when you didn't call or even show up at the office, that was what you wanted.''

He had no idea how she leaped from A to B. ''I was working. I had to go to Los Angeles at a moment's notice.''

Did he think she was a mind reader? ''You could have told me.''

She was right, he should have. But he had his reasons. ''I wanted to tell you in person.''

Mindy didn't understand. It made no sense. ''That you were working?''

''That I wanted to marry you.''

Everything around her evaporated. ''What?''

He'd botched it, he thought in frustration. She deserved better. ''That didn't come out any better than an e-mail, did it?''

She didn't think she could love him any more than she did right at this moment. ''You're not being graded for sentence structure, Jason, just content.'' She searched his face. ''If you're serious.''

He pulled her to him. ''Haven't you noticed, I'm a very serious man.''

Mindy threaded her arms around his neck. ''Prove it.''

He brought his mouth down to hers and kissed her, completely oblivious to the cheers that went up around them. New Yorkers were suckers for a live performance. They always had been.

Epilogue

"Am I too late?"

Jason burst breathlessly into the birthing room, having just run down the length of the hall to reach it. He'd all but driven his car onto the sidewalk in an effort to arrive at the hospital as quickly as possible. Jason had jumped into his car the moment he'd gotten Mindy's call.

All he could think of was that she was a week early.

If he'd known that she was going to pull something like this, he would never have left her this morning. He would have stayed at her side instead of having her take a taxicab to get to the hospital.

What if she'd given birth in the back seat?

He didn't want to think about it.

Dr. Cross looked utterly unfazed by the fact that he was about to bring twins into the world, Jason thought grudgingly. The man smiled at him, as if attempting to put him at ease.

As if that was possible.

"No, you're just in time, Mr. Mallory. Although I'm tempted to say just barely." He looked at his patient. "This may go down as the fastest labor on record." Mindy Mallory had called Manhattan Multiples less than an hour ago. By the time she'd arrived at the hospital, she was already dilated to eight centimeters. She was approaching ten with a breathtaking speed.

Jason took Mindy's hand. She looked so small lying there. "What do you want me to do?" The question was directed toward the doctor, but he was looking at Mindy as he asked.

Mindy wound her fingers around his hand. The pain hadn't been as bad as she'd anticipated, but it wasn't exactly a picnic, either. And it kept shooting through her at an accelerating rate. It was almost constant now.

"Just...be here..." she told him. "Like...you've been...for...the past six...months."

"I'm not going anywhere." He bent over and kissed her forehead. "But you might be."

He was such a worrier. Who would have ever thought? "I...have no...intention...of dying, Jason. Women...give...birth to twins...every...day."

He shook his head. The thought of losing her hadn't been allowed to enter his head. He wouldn't have been able to think of life without her.

"No, I meant after you give birth." He was going to save this until she was in recovery, but he knew she'd want to know. "I talked to that managing editor I told you about. The one at the *Times.*" God, could a man love a woman more than he loved her right at this moment? He didn't think so. "He said to come in anytime you're ready and he'd see where he could start you off."

Mindy blinked. Despite the cool room, perspiration was dripping into her eyes. She was trying not to twist about from the pain, but it wasn't easy. She stared at Jason, his news penetrating the wall of immense discomfort closing in around her. "You're...serious. You're...not...just saying that...to get my...mind... off the...pain?"

His heart ached to see her like this, but she'd absolutely refused to have a C-section. "I don't think anything could do that." He held her hand up to his lips and kissed it. "And yes, I'm serious. Tricia and Wyatt are going to have to share you with the *New York Times*—and me."

"Dana...and...Joshua," she corrected. They still hadn't decided on names. The debate was going hot and heavy, but they'd managed to narrow the field down some. "But...we'll...talk." And then her eyes flew open, startled. Frightened. She stared at her draped lower half. "Oh God…I think…company… has…*ARRIVED*."

Jason's hand tightened around hers, as if he could channel some of her pain. He looked toward the doctor. Dr. Cross was repositioning himself at the foot of the gurney. The nurse Jason vaguely recognized from somewhere was at the doctor's elbow.

Everything happened so fast after that, it was hard for Jason to properly recall the order. It seemed like one moment he was propping Mindy up, helping her to breathe, to push, and the next moment, with each effort she put forth, another infant appeared.

And then the doctor was stripping off his mask, shaking his head and smiling broadly.

"Amazing," was all the man could say.

The word, Jason thought as he took his newborn daughter into his arms and looked at Mindy holding their son, fit the occasion rather perfectly.

Amazing.

* * * * *

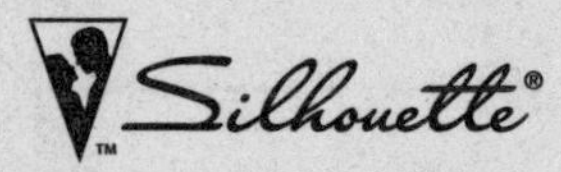

SPECIAL EDITION®

COMING NEXT MONTH

#1555 DANIEL'S DESIRE—Sherryl Woods
The Devaneys
Though he hadn't expected a second chance at happiness, that's exactly what Daniel Devaney got when he came face-to-face with his ex, Molly Creighton. Though a tragic loss had torn them asunder, *this* time Daniel was determined to fight for the love that burned stronger than ever.

#1556 PRINCE AND FUTURE...DAD?—Christine Rimmer
Viking Brides
The princess was pregnant! And the king had every intention of making sure his daughter married the father of her unborn child. But Princess Liv Thorson had other plans, and they didn't include marrying the notorious playboy Prince Finn. Or so she told herself....

#1557 QUINN'S WOMAN—Susan Mallery
Hometown Heartbreakers
Ex-Special Forces agent Quinn Reynolds agreed to share his skills with self-defense instructor D. J. Monroe. But their sessions triggered as many sparks as punches. Fighting the love growing between them might only be a losing battle!

#1558 MARRY ME...AGAIN—Cheryl St.John
Montana Mavericks: The Kingsleys
Ranch foreman Devlin "Devil" Holmes had wild ways not even getting married could tame...until Brynna decided to leave him. Being without her was torture. Could he convince Brynna their marriage deserved a second chance?

#1559 THE FERTILITY FACTOR—Jennifer Mikels
Manhattan Multiples
Nurse Lara Mancini struggled with the possibility that she might be infertile. But her feelings for handsome Dr. Derek Cross were quickly escalating. Would he want to pursue a relationship knowing she might be unable to conceive?

#1560 FOUND IN LOST VALLEY—Laurie Paige
Seven Devils
He wasn't who she thought he was. Seth Dalton, successful attorney, wasn't *really* a Dalton. Amelia Miller was a good woman who deserved a good man, not a fraud. The fact that he was falling for her didn't change a thing...but her love for him—that could be enough to change *everything*.

SSECNM0703